SINGING
FROM THE
WELL

ALSO BY

REINALDO ARENAS

Hallucinations
El Central
Farewell to the Sea

SINGING FROM THE WELL

REINALDO ARENAS

TRANSLATED BY
ANDREW HURLEY

VIKING

VIKING
Viking Penguin Inc., 40 West 23rd Street, New York, New York 10010, U.S.A.
Penguin Books Ltd, 27 Wrights Lane, London W8 5TZ (Publishing & Editorial),
and Harmondsworth, Middlesex, England (Distribution & Warehouse)
Penguin Books Australia Ltd, Ringwood, Victoria, Australia
Penguin Books Canada Limited, 2801 John Street, Markham, Ontario, Canada L3R 1B4
Penguin Books (N.Z.) Ltd, 182–190 Wairau Road, Auckland 10, New Zealand

First published in 1987 by Viking Penguin Inc.
Published simultaneously in Canada
First published in Spain by Editorial Argos Vergara, S.A.,
as *Cantando en el pozo*
Copyright © Reinaldo Arenas, 1982

Acknowledgment is made for permission to translate
and publish the following copyrighted material:
Epigraph on page vii from *Luna de Enfrente*, by Jorge Luis Borges. Copyright
© 1925 by Jorge Luis Borges. By permission of the estate of
Jorge Luis Borges and Emece Editores.
Epigraph on page ix by Federico García Lorca. By permission of Thomas Colchie
Associates, Inc., as agents for the estate of Federico García Lorca.
Epigraph on page 83 from *Ficciones*, by Jorge Luis Borges. Copyright © 1944
by Jorge Luis Borges. By permission of the estate of
Jorge Luis Borges and Emece Editores.

LIBRARY OF CONGRESS CATALOGING IN PUBLICATION DATA
Arenas, Reinaldo, 1943–
Singing from the well.
Translation of: Celestino antes del alba.
I. Title.
PQ7390.A72C413   1987   863   85-41092
ISBN 0-670-80805-9

Printed in the United States of America by
The Book Press, Brattleboro, Vermont
Set in Trump Medieval
Designed by The Sarabande Press

For Maricela Cordovez,
the prettiest girl in the world

*But no man dared look upon his
face, for it was like the
face of an angel.*
                    Oscar Wilde

*Dawn will break on my tight-squeezed
eyelids.*
                    Jorge Luis Borges

Blessed are those whose lives unfold in wings,
The butterflies, and those on whom the moonbeams fall,
Blessed are those who pluck the rose of spring,
And those who harvest wheat.

Blessed are those who doubt Death's fatal knell,
For having now sweet Paradise's song,
And blessed the wind that bloweth where it will
And knoweth the infinite is sweet.

Blessed are the glorious and the strong,
Victors self-charmed against compassion's sting,
And blessed too those blessed and smiled upon
Gathered at gentle Francis' feet.

We have known hard times.
We have walked many a road.
We have sought to understand the word
Soughed by the aspen tree.

Federico García Lorca

SINGING FROM THE WELL

There went my mother, she just went running out the door. She was screaming like a crazy woman that she was going to jump down the well. I see my mother at the bottom of the well. I see her floating in the greenish water choked with leaves. So I run for the yard, out to where the well is, that's fenced around with a wellhead of naked-boy saplings so rickety it's almost falling in.

I run up and peek over. But just like always—the only one down there is me. Me being reflected from way down there up to me above. Me—and I disappear if you so much as spit into the oozy green water.

Madre mía, Mama! This is not the first time you've tricked me—every day you say you're going to jump headfirst down the well, but *ha!* You never do it. You think you're going to drive me crazy, making me run these wild-goose chases from the house to the well and the well to the house. Well, no. I'm getting tired of this. If you're not going to jump, it's all right with me. But don't say you're going to jump and then not do it.

We're out here crying, behind the old thicket of prickly wild pineapples. My mother and I, we're crying. The lizards are so big in this pineapple thicket! You ought to see them! The lizards here are in all different shapes. I just saw one with two heads. Two heads on that lizard slithering along.

Most of these lizards know me, and they hate me. I know they hate me, and they're just waiting for the day . . . Bastards!, I say to them, and I dry my eyes. And then I pick up a stick and go for them. But they know a lot more than you'd give them credit for, and the second they see me stop crying they run into the thicket, and they disappear. What really makes me mad is that I know that all the time I can't see them and I'm thrashing around looking for them, to try to catch them, they're watching me. They're probably laughing at me.

Finally I catch one. I whack him with the stick and break him in half. But he's still alive, and one half runs off while the other piece jumps up and down in front of me like it was saying, You little crybaby, don't think you can kill me *that* easy . . .

"You beast!" says my mother to me, and she throws a rock at me and hits me in the head. "Let those poor lizards live in peace!" My head has split into two halves and one of them has run off. The other half, though, stays there in front of my mother. Dancing. Dancing. Dancing.

Now all of us are dancing, up here on the roof of the house. What a lot of people on the roof! I love to climb up onto the palm branches of the thatch, and I always find one or two nests of shiny little green-and-purple blackbirds up here. I don't eat the blackbirds' eggs, because people say they're always rotten, so what I do is throw them at my grandfather's head, because every time he sees me up on top of the house he picks up the long pole he uses to cut off palm leaves way up on the tree and he starts poking at me like I was a bunch of coconuts. One of the eggs has splattered in my grandfather's eye, and I'm not sure, but it looks to me like it put his eye out. One-eyed Grandpa.

But no—you'd have to poke that old coot's eyes out with a spear, because his eyeballs are tougher than the bottom of a bucket.

Dancing all by myself on the roof. I made my cousins get down, and now they're asleep under the pine trees. Inside the white brick wall. And the crosses.

"What are there so many crosses for?" I asked Mama the day we went to see my cousins.

"It's so they'll rest in peace and go to heaven," my mother told me, while she cried her eyes out and stole a fresh wreath off one of the crosses a little way away. So I pulled up seven crosses and carried them home with me under my arm. And I kept them in bed with me, so that way I could sleep when I went to bed and not even feel the mosquitoes, and mosquitoes here have worse stingers than scorpions.

"These crosses are so I can sleep," I told my grandmother when she came into my room. My grandmother is an old, old woman, I thought, while I squatted under the bed. "Take these crosses for you," I told Grandma, handing her the crosses. But she carried them *all* off. "We've got a shortage of firewood today," she said. And when she got to the cookstove she chopped them into kindling and threw them in the fire.

"What have you done with my crosses, you old nanny goat!" I said, and I grabbed a piece of smoking cross and went at her. I was going to poke out her eyes. But that old biddy wasn't born yesterday, and when I picked up the burning stick she grabbed the pot of scalding water that was on top of the cookstove and threw it on me. If I hadn't jumped back I'd have been cooked alive. "Don't fool with me," said Grandma, and then she gave me a roasted sweet potato to eat. I took the half-eaten sweet potato out to the bileweed patch and I dug a hole there and I put it in the ground. Then I made a cross out of a dry bileweed plant and put it in the ground, too, next to the dead sweet potato.

But now I better stop thinking about those things and see about getting down off the roof without Grandpa running me through with the pole. I know—I'll slip down the zinc rain gutters like I was a cat, and when he's not looking I'll jump out of the rain gutter and run off. Oh, I wish I could jump on top of my grandfather and squash him! Everything is all his fault. *His* fault. That's why I and all my cousins all meet here. Up here on the roof of the house. Like we've done so many times—we have to plan a way to have Grandpa die before his time.

This house has always been a hell. Even before everybody died all anybody ever talked about was dead people. And more dead people. And Grandma outprayed everybody, crossing herself in every corner of the house. But when things got really bad was when Celestino took it into his head to write poems. Poor Celestino! I can see him now—sitting on the parlor doorsill beam and pulling off his arms.

Poor Celestino! Writing. Writing and writing and writing, and never stopping, even on the spines of the account books where Grandpa writes down the dates the cows got pregnant. On yucca leaves and even on the hard round husks of the palm trees the horses didn't get there soon enough to eat.

Writing. Writing. And when not a single yucca leaf is left to mess up—or a single palm leaf husk, or Grandpa's ledger books—Celestino starts writing on the trunks of the trees.

"That's what girls do," said my mother, when she found out Celestino had got it into his head to start writing. And that was the first time she jumped down the well.

4

"I'd rather die than have a son like that," and the water level in the well rose.

Mama was so fat in those days! Really really fat. So when she dived into the water it came way up. You ought to have seen it! I ran out to the well and I could wash my hands in the water and I got a drink almost without bending over. I just stretched out my neck a little. And then I started drinking, using my two hands like they were dippers. The water was so cool and clear! I love drinking out of my hands and getting them all wet. Like birds do. But of course, since birds don't have hands, they drink with their beaks . . . What if they did have hands, though, and we were the ones that were mixed up? . . . I don't even know what to say. In this house things have gone from bad to worse— I don't even know, really and truly, what to think. But I still think anyway. And worry. And think. And worry . . . And now Celestino comes up to me again with all the palm branches under his arms and the carpenter's pencils sticking out the middle of his stomach.

"Celestino! Celestino!"
"Carmelina's child has gone crazy!"
"He's gone crazy! He's gone crazy!"
"He's scribbling on the trunks of the trees!"
"He's batty as a loon!"
"What a disgrace! My God! This kind of thing could only happen to me!"
"What a disgrace!"

We went down to the river. The boys' voices kept getting louder and louder, and finally they were yelling. They pushed Celestino out of the water and told him to go swim with the women. I got out of the water too, right behind Celestino, and then the boys caught me and kicked my behind eight times— four on each side. I felt like I wanted to cry. But he cried for me too.

And night caught us in the middle of the pasture. Boom, just like that, night falls around here. Just when you'd least expect it, here it comes. It wraps all around us and then it won't go away. The sun almost never comes up here. Oh, of course a lot of people say the sun comes up, or morning comes. I say the same thing once in a while.

"When we get to the house, don't let them find out what the boys did," Celestino said, and he dried his eyes with a guava leaf. But when we got to the house they were already waiting for us at the door. Nobody said a word. Not a peep. We came to the house, went into the dining room, and at that, she ran out through the kitchen door. She gave a shriek behind the cookstove and started running all over the yard, and finally she jumped down the well again . . . When I was littler, Grandma gave me a hen and told me, "Follow her till you find her nest, and don't come back to this house till your pockets are full of eggs." I turned the hen loose in the middle of the yard. She took off. She flapped her wings and flew three circles in the air. And she disappeared, cackling through the thicket of wild pineapples.

"The hen got away from me, Grandma."
"Son of a bitch! We'd all be better off if you just died!"

Celestino came up to me and put his hand on my head. I was so sad. It was the first time anybody had ever cursed at me. I was so sad I started crying. Celestino lifted me up in the air, and he said to me, "What foolishness, but you might as well get used to it." I looked at Celestino, and I realized that he was crying too, but he was trying not to show it. So that made me realize that he still hadn't got used to it either. I stopped crying a second. And the two of us went out into the yard. It was still daylight.

It was still daylight.

. . .

There had been a rainstorm. But the lightning bolts hadn't been satisfied with just that, so they kept on winking and flashing behind the clouds and way up in the highest leaves of the shower-of-gold bushes. What a nice smell there is after it rains . . . I had never noticed things like that before. Now I did. So I took air in through my nose and mouth, both. And then I filled my stomach up again with the smell and the air. The sun wasn't going to come back out anymore now, there were too many clouds. But it was still light out. We walked along under the sugar apple trees, and I could feel the mud with leaves all mixed up in it coming up through the holes in my shoes. The mud was cold, and all of a sudden I got the idea of playing like I was walking through snow and that the sugar apple trees were Christmas trees and pines and evergreens and that the whole family was in the house buzzing and clattering and laughing, which up to then I'd never heard before. "What a shame there's no snow here where we live," I said to Celestino. But he wasn't with me anymore. "Celestino! Celestino!" I called, very very softly, trying not to wake myself up and find myself in the middle of a mud puddle.

Celestino! Celestino!

The lightning bolts came back again. My mother ran across the snow and hugged me tight. And she said "son" to me. I smiled at my mother, and then I jumped and hugged her around the neck. And the two of us started to dance on the ground, all dressed in white. At that, the noise of the people singing and making such a hubbub in the house got closer and closer to us; they were coming towards us with a whole roast pig on a spit, and they were singing all the way. All my cousins made a chorus and danced around us in a ring. Mama lifted me way up in the air. As high as her arms could reach. And from up there I could see the sky getting darker and darker, and a shower bigger and whiter than the one that had come down before starting to work its way out of the clouds. So I wiggled out of my mother's arms and ran over to where my cousins were, and we started jumping up and down in the snow as high as we could and we sang and sang and sang, and little by little we turned transparent—as transparent as the snow that didn't get mixed up with the mud, it just spread out white and pure and clean no matter how much we jumped around.

For one second there was a great big loud clap of thunder. I saw the lightning melt every bit of the snow as quick as you could snap your fingers. And before I could yell and close my eyes, I saw myself—walking through a big mud puddle—and saw Celestino writing poems on the sugar apple trees, and their bark is as hard as iron. And my grandfather came out of the kitchen with a hatchet and started cutting down all the trees Celestino had written on, even if it was just one word.

I watched him swinging his hatchet, whacking away at the tree trunks, and I said to myself, "The time has come. I'm going to break his back with a rock." But I didn't. What if I miss and it doesn't kill him? If the rock doesn't hit him just right, then I'm done for, because Grandpa will jump on me like a mad dog and make mincemeat out of me with the hatchet.

There's not a thing I can do all by myself. Sometimes there are a whole lot of things I wish I could do. But I don't do a single solitary thing. One day I told myself I was going to set the house on fire. I climbed up one of the forked props for the wall, up to the roof, and I had already struck the match and all I had to do was hold it to the palm thatch for the whole house and everything to go up like gunpowder, and not a black smudge of what had been the house be left, and all of a sudden I remembered the baby blackbirds. They had just pecked out of their shells and they were asleep all nice and still in the nest over by the rain gutters. I remembered them and that made me feel so sad. So I didn't do it. I didn't do a thing. I got down off the roof saying to myself, "Well, when the baby blackbirds grow up and fly away from the nest I'll set fire to the house, and there won't be any problem with doing it then at all." And when I got to the ground I felt the hard crack of a big thick switch that rattled my ribs and almost broke my back.

"Son of a bitch! I told you not to climb up on the roof of the house—it stops raining faster outside than it does inside these days, with you climbing all over the thatch and shinnying down the rain gutters all the time and punching holes in the roof. You goose! Get to work!"

And another crack. And another. And another. Grandpa had been waiting for me, just biding his time, under the rainspout, and he had taken such good aim when I was climbing down that there was no way I could duck the switch cracking and then cracking again, going "psssst-ch!" through the air from the mad blind rage Grandpa was taking out on my back. The stinking old coot! He caught me by surprise, and I didn't know what to do when I saw that switch coming at me. Something just came over me, and I really felt like crying. But then I started getting so mad, so mad inside that I bet I even turned all different colors and everything. So at that I gave a great big huge scream and ran for the meadow on the mountainside as fast as I could go, with the old coot after me, cursing and muttering and stumbling over the tree stumps he had cut down his own evil self. The high meadow is so beautiful! I love it.

When I got there I jumped into the first clump of tall grass I could find. And I didn't even feel the chiggers biting me, or even the ticks there are on the mountain. I lay on my back and made myself as comfortable as I could and watched the clouds. And I started eating some little wild persimmons I could just reach and pull off from a persimmon tree. Two great big clouds ran into each other and smashed into a million pieces.

The pieces fell on my house and squashed it, right down to the ground. I never thought pieces of cloud would be so big and heavy. They're sharp as a knife, too. One of them just sliced my grandfather's head right off. My cousins were down at the river, so they managed to escape. Not hide nor hair of my grandmother has been found, so I guess the clouds broke her to smithereens and ants came and carried off the pieces. I run down from the high meadow to the house, buried under the rubble of clouds, and when I get there all I can see is one of my mother's arms and one of Celestino's. My mother's arm is moving a little in the rubble and soot and ashes. (Because in this house the smoke from the cookstove has no place to go, because there's just one window and it's in the dining room, so that's why the house is always as black as the bottom of a kettle.)

"Get me out of here, I'm suffocating!" the voice of my mother tells me, and her arm waves around and jumps and twitches.

I can't hear Celestino say a word. Not a peep. His arm is barely sticking out of the soot and ashes and palm branches, and it's moving so very very slow and still that it's almost like his hand is petting the beams and the pieces of black thatch that have buried him alive.

"Get me out of here, goddammit! I'm your mother!"
"I'll be right there. I'll be right there!"
And I smile as I go over to where Celestino's still, cold hand is, and I start lifting up the big boulders of cloud from on top of him. Until finally, at just about nightfall, I've finally got him free.

The storm of clouds has let up a little, and a fine fine shower is little by little turning everything an almost transparent white white color. Out of that mist of water just barely barely falling I see my mother coming towards me carrying the ox prod in her hands. Sharpened to a fine point.
The chiggers have almost eaten my whole back, but I didn't feel them biting me, I was in such a daze. My mother walks right

We went out to pick
      STAR APPLES,
but the only thing we
could find was some
guavas, and they
weren't ripe yet.

— MY GRANDMOTHER

across the top of the wild pineapple thicket, not even watching out for thorns, and then she takes off flying.

Now she's right in front of me. In the middle of the high meadow, and pointing the prod straight at my throat.

"Why didn't you save me? You jackass!"

Mama grips the prod tighter, and I can feel a cold tickle that starts going right through the skin of my throat.

"I am your mother."

My cousin Eulogia got lost in this meadow one time. Poor Eulogia! She went out to get firewood and she never came back to the house again. With or without the firewood.

"Answer me—why didn't you save me, if I'm the woman that brought you into the world!"

Something must have happened to my cousin Eulogia that she still hasn't come back. We all waited for her in the dining room, not saying a word to one another. Looking at the floor or out the only window. But not saying a single word to one another.

Eulogia!
Eulogia!

Grandma cries because she says she knows that if Eulogia's lost Grandpa will hang himself. I feel sorry for Eulogia. But if that's true about Grandpa then I'd be very happy if she were to get lost.

"You're no son of mine! What you are is a beast!"

Hail Mary, full of grace. Blessed be the fruit of thy womb. Virgin Mary, please let Eulogia show up, because if she doesn't I'll pitch you into that cookstove . . .

Our Father, Who art in heaven . . .

"You beast! You beast! Instead of saving your own mother, you'd let her suffocate in that ash heap."

Poor Eulogia . . . When she went off to the mountain I saw that she was crying. She had just come out of Grandpa's room. Poor Eulogia! If she wasn't the goose she is she wouldn't have let Grandpa get up on top of her like he did. But she's the slave for this whole house and everybody gets on top of her. And does whatever they want to her. Even me. One afternoon I tripped her and pulled her down out behind the bileweed patch and got up on top of her. She didn't make the slightest peep. She brayed like a mule when you give it three or four slaps with a stick of wood, and she broke out in big drops of sweat.

Poor Eulogia! She left the house crying while Grandma was throwing the biggest fit you ever saw. As soon as she turned her back Mama slushed the dirty dishwater on her head.

"Goddamn you! My only son, and he's turned out to be as thick as a mule! Was there ever a sadder fate than mine! I *knew* I should've died before I came into the world!"

It's as plain as day that Eulogia didn't really get lost on the mountain, like my whole family would like me to think. And if she didn't, then they'll see—one day we'll find her hanging from a tree with a vine around her neck, hanging almost as high as the parson birds, and they *never* come down to the ground, except to get a drink of water, maybe, when they can't find a drop on the leaves of the trees and they're so thirsty they can't even fly. If it weren't for that, they'd never *ever* come down!

What I wouldn't give to be a parson bird! I wouldn't drink water even if my throat got as dry as a rock.

The point of the prod goes in very very cool right through my throat. I hang on to the rocks and grass for dear life and I can feel that coolness all the way to my tonsils.

I wish I could escape.

Except really, I'm not so sure I do. And I think, If they let me go I'd tell Mama to stab me again with the stick. I would— I'd even get down on my knees to her and beg her to do it; and tell her to make the stick sharper, too.

"Goddamn you! Goddamn you!"

As the cool feeling fills my whole throat I gradually realize that my mother isn't mean. I look at her, standing over me, and she looks like a giant, or like a great big huge crepe myrtle bush like the ones people tie animals to. Never noticing that the crepe myrtle is all dried up from so many reins and ropes being tied around it.

My mother gets prettier and prettier and prettier. How beautiful! She's so pretty in her burlap-bag skirt and the big blouse she stole from Eulogia. I love my mother and I know she's good and that she loves me. I have never seen my mother. But I always picture her like she is now—crying and running her fingers over my throat in the coolest, nicest tickling way you can imagine.

I should picture her like that, not the other way.

"You miserable child! What I really ought to do is hang myself this very instant!"

I feel like getting up and hugging her. Telling her I'm sorry and carrying her off far away where neither Grandma nor Grandpa could ever bother us anymore. I feel like saying, "Madre mía! Madre mía, Mama! You're so pretty today with that honeysuckle in your hair! You look like one of those women that you only see on Christmas cards. Let's get out of here, let's leave right this second. Let's get our things together and just take off. Let's not stay another minute in this horrible horrible house that looks like the bottom of a kettle. Let's leave now, before that jackass of a grandfather wakes up and makes us get out of bed and milk the cows."

"Let's leave right this minute, because in the daytime we won't be able to get away."

"Madre mía! Madre mía!"

But I don't say another single word. What I was planning to say got stuck in my throat. It hit the point of the stick that ran all the way through me now. And it didn't come out my mouth. For a second my mother stood there paralyzed—listening to me. The whole high meadow knows now that I said *my mother*. The whole hill knows it too, and now it repeats it in a very very strange echo that's almost as close as my own voice.

Mama just stands there with her mouth open. She pulls the prod out of my throat. She throws it into the grass. She puts her hands to her face and lets out a huge huge wail.
Huge.

And she takes off flying, across the old thicket of wild pineapples and into the house, through those big holes in the roof that I've made climbing up and down looking for baby blackbirds or meeting my dead cousins.

I don't know what to do. My throat stings like the dickens. I run my hand over it and it turns out it's nothing. Not even a scratch. The fire ants have eaten my whole back away and the chiggers are starting to get on my face. My mother has disappeared and it's getting to be almost night now. I wish I could make it to the house without anybody seeing me and without her starting to poke me with the prod again or Grandma throwing scalding water on my back.

"You can, you can. Tonight you can," a band of blackbirds tells me, flying over way up high, all in rows, one after another. But how in the world could those blackbirds have been talking to me! I don't believe it. I look up at the sky again, and the black line of their wings is as straight and perfect as could be—the birds' trip has just gone right on and I'll never find out the truth.

Then I start crying.

I like to walk at night, when nobody can see me. I do. I like to because that's when I can hop on just one foot. Get up on a tree stump and spread out my arms and let myself go and dance on it, with my arms out to keep my balance. Do all kinds of somersaults and tricks, and all of them different. Roll around on the ground and take off running again, until I disappear into the fog and in the branches of the Indian laurel tree, which is still standing. I like to be by myself and just break out singing. Celestino has come up to me and asked me for a drink of water. Where from. "Where from," I ask him, and I hold out my empty hands. But the real truth is that I have a terrible memory and I can never remember a song. And so that's why I make them up. I almost like making them up better than learning them by heart.

I'm making one up now.

I hope nobody hears me, because I don't know if this song is any good. I hope nobody hears me, because I'd hate for them to hear me. How embarrassing if my cousins were to surprise me singing made-up songs and hopping through the tree stumps! How embarrassing it would be if somebody heard me!

Then it was my mother who came to ask me for some water. She said to me, "The well has dried up. What am I going to do now—I'm about to die of thirst." I didn't answer her. I held out my wet hands to her, but then I stuck them in my pants pockets again. Now everything has turned almost transparent. Tonight things look so pretty to me. Are they really that way, I wonder. Or is it that I look at things differently than anybody else does? I don't know. But anyway, even if, as my mother says, this is the ugliest place on the face of the earth, *I* don't think it is—there are a lot of very pretty things. Take the house—that I'd like to set fire to sometimes—I know it's not ugly, and even if it's falling down and the hens drop their droppings on it every single night (because the damned hens sleep up on the roof), there are spots where not a drop of hen shit falls, and everything looks nice. Except people say that's not true—that there's not a spot you can breathe in in this house. But there is—sometimes, when I'm really really in a fury, I go off into the corner of the breezeway, where once upon a time there was a big window with an iron grating but now there's just the grating in the wall. I go off to that corner, under the nest the mad wasps built. And I sit in the corner of the breezeway. I stay there keeping very very still, not making any noise, hardly moving at all, so as not to stir up the wasps. And I start feeling peaceful. I don't know how that could be. Maybe it's because it's a place full of green leaves. Because the ivy in this corner has grown all over the walls and the monkey puzzle bush is bigger than I am now. Uh-huh, that must be why, because there are a lot of plants and you almost get lost in all the leaves and stalks and branches and you start feeling better. And when it rains, that corner of the breezeway is even prettier, because the tulip cups fill up with water and when you shake them the water falls on you, so cold and fresh you'd swear it was pellets of sleet. One time Grandma stood under the cups of the tulips and I shook them. And a freezing downpour came down right on her head. Thank goodness I took off running, because if I hadn't that miserable thankless grandmother of mine would have planted me right there next to the tulips . . . She got so mad she wanted to cut the plants off at the ground. But just then

Grandpa was coming in from the mountain. And just to be contrary (because he doesn't care one whit about the plants, it's all the same to him whether there's a tulip or a poisonwood tree in the breezeway), Grandpa told her, "You better not touch those plants." And that started them off fighting again. So since then Grandma has taken such a dislike to those flowers in the breezeway that she grits her teeth every time she goes by them. And one day I saw her throw scalding water on the tulips so they would dry up. So I ran and told Grandpa, and he grabbed her by the bun on the back of her head and dragged her all the way to the cookstove and grabbed both her hands and stuck them in the water that was bubbling away in the pot. Grandma caught her breath, like a cow when you kick her in the chest. But she never threw scalding water on the plants in the breezeway again. So now I can roll around in the leaves in peace, and sometimes I feel so good there that I scratch up the roots of the tulips and eat them! Tulip bulbs are so good to eat! They're always cold and they taste like bitter marmalade, and I get drunk from them. They make me feel so happy that in no time I'm asleep in the leaves blown into the corner. Except sometimes the wasps get all stirred up, up there in the wasp-nest, and they coil themselves up and drop down on my face and even sting me two or three times and everything. But that's just sometimes. The rest of the times nothing happens to me and I can sleep as peaceful as you please for two or three hours . . . This place does have some very pretty things! Take the people—they're not as ugly as they say they are. My own mother, that sometimes behaves like such a mad dog, there are times she's different . . . I still remember one day when I was coming back from the well with the two buckets of water over my shoulder. Just as I was coming to the house I slipped and fell down. And that made me so sad that the only thing I could do was roll over and over in the mud puddle it made on the ground, and start to cry. And my mother, who had been watching me from the kitchen door, walked out to where I was, and I said to myself, "Now I'm in for it." But she didn't do a thing. Except squat down in the loblolly and run her hand slowly slowly over my head, like she was smoothing and straightening out my hair—it's always such a tangled mess that Grandpa says

I look like an upside-down broom. I was surprised. I looked at my mother and I'm not sure, because it was still early early in the morning and there was a lot of fog, I'm not absolutely sure but it looked to me like she was crying . . . From that time on whenever I fall down with the water buckets on the way back, I just lie there very still and I wait for her. Except sometimes I'm wrong, and instead of running her hands over my head what she does is crack a stick over it. But no matter what happens, I will never be able to get it out of my head, the way it happened that one time. I always picture her squatting down beside me in the loblolly and running her hand over my head while her eyes get shinier and shinier through the big fog that covers this whole part of the country in the mornings . . . That's another one of the things I like about this part of the country—the fog. So white . . . You can stretch your hands out and not see them, almost. And if I do see them, they look so white they don't even look like my own hands . . . Even Grandpa, who's practically black from all the sun he gets—when it's morning I watch him walk through the pasture and he looks a little bit like a giant, he's so white-looking through the fog. That's why every single day I get up first thing in the morning and come out here and walk up to the highest spot in the pasture, where the mango trees are, and I sit for hours and hours almost in a daze, watching how pretty the house is, covered with fog, because it's almost like one of those story houses. Those that you only read about in books like the one Celestino was carrying the first day he showed up at the house, scared and hanging on to his dead mother's arm . . . And not till the sun is thi-i-i-is big and starts frying you to a crisp do things stop looking pretty. It's a shame, really it is, that you can't always live in this fog, because that way things would always be different and my grandfather would always be a white old man. Damp and happy. Walking through the grass, and it white too. And the house—if only the sun would never come out—would be a story house like the one on the cover of Celestino's book, and who knows but that even my mother, instead of whacking me with a fence post every now and then, might always run her hand over my head, because you have to remember that the day she really did do it there was a lot of fog . . . Uh-huh, I think it's the sun's fault—with that great huge glare of his—I think it's all the sun's fault that things turn so ugly and people start acting like mad dogs over the least little thing. That's the reason I want winter to get here so much. Except winter is so short here that it comes and goes and we can barely tell the difference. But I wish it *would* come, even for just one day—so I could slip and fall with the water buckets again . . .

It's midnight already. Maybe tomorrow there'll be a big fog.

"Don't you cut down that Indian laurel tree! I've got me a nice safe place all set up there!" screams my grandmother at my grandfather, who by now has cut down almost all the trees Celestino has made a single mark on.

"What do you mean, don't cut it down! That goddamned young jackass has covered it with all these peculiar words!"

"Stop it! Leave that tree alone! That's the only thing that keeps the lightning off this house!"

"If you knew how to read you wouldn't tell me not to cut it down, I'll tell you!"

"I said to leave it alone! Drop that hatchet!"

"You hush if you don't want me to split your skull with it!"

Grandma and Grandpa have started in again. They both hang on to the hatchet and neither one will give up. Old jackasses, the both of them! With any luck the hatchet will whack one of them and stick in their belly. Fat chance! Those two old coots are tougher than a whetstone. "A hundred years I plan to live," says Grandpa every night, to strip the rest of us of any hope we might have. "And I'll be the one to bury you," my grandmother says back to him every time. So there's no hope for Mama and me. And the saddest part of it is that it's true—Grandma and Grandpa both are as healthy as a wild mule, and I don't figure they would die if a lightning bolt fell on them. Old jackasses! They'd hang on for dear life not just to a straw, they'd grab a red-hot poker. Before they'd give up.

"I ate raw sweet potato for more than two months."

"I gave birth to my second daughter in the river. The freshet carried her away, but not me—there's not the freshet yet that could carry me away."

"Of the twelve of us men that went down into the mine, the only one to come out again was me. The others helped me to get out. But as soon as I crawled out I took off running. You don't know how dangerous it is to help somebody that's as good as dead! You almost always wind up dead yourself. But I thought things over and took off running. And here I am, standing before you!"

A horse has shot out from behind the house and galloped off and disappeared into the fog. I see him fade into the thicket of whiteness and little by little I start feeling very very happy. Except I can't say why.

Has he been carving on the tree trunks! If I knew how to read I'd know what it is he's written on all those trees. It must be something awfully important. It must be something extra-specially important because while he's writing he doesn't even hear the lightning striking right around his ears.

"Where are you going with that child?"

"To school. I won't have him be a barbarian like you people, or go hungry like I have."

"Like taking a mule to school to teach him to play the flute."

"That just shows how mean and evil people can be, you see—not wanting you to prosper. But you're going to study. Do you hear me!—study, or I'll break your head open and stuff the learning in myself."

What a lot of boys and girls there are in this school. And the only one with his mother in tow is me. How humiliating! . . .

. . .

BAH,
LET'S MAKE ALL THE
GRIMACES
WE CAN.

— Arthur
Rimbaud

"Look. That kid came to school on his mother's apron strings."

"He looks like one of those plantain-eating hoot owls."

"And his mother looks like a lizard!"

"Lizard's kid! Lizard's kid!"

"I'll leave you here with the teacher. I've told you, now—do what she tells you."

"Now you've got him! Hit 'im! Hit 'im now!"

"Kill that little hoot owl!"

"Kill the hoot owl!"

"He cries like a girl!"

"The lizard's kid is crying like a girl!"

"Cut from the same cloth as Celestino—pants outside, but petticoats underneath!"

"He's Celestino's cousin!"

"His cousin! His cousin!"

"Hit 'im now!"

"Open his mouth!"

"Stuff this horse shit down his throat!"

"Celestino the crazy kid's cousin! He's Celestino's cousin, the one that writes poetry on the trunks of the trees!"

"They're both queers!"

"Queers!"

"Make him eat that horse flop!"

"Button your pants, boys!"

"The boys at school have beat you up again! You sissy! Don't you have any arms to defend yourself with? Such a big boy and such a goose! The next time you come home all beat up and your clothes with shit all over them I'm the one that's going to finish the job, so you stop being such a ninny."

"Here comes Celestino's cousin again. Let's get 'im down and kick 'im . . ."

. . .

"What in the world *happened* to you! What mud puddle have you been rolling around in! And you smell like human shit! Who was it that shit on your head? Answer me! Unless you want me to whip the answer out of you with the machete scabbard! Who did this to you? . . . How could this happen to me! I've always said I should've just died before I was born in this godforsaken place! Shit! I'm sick and tired! One of these days I'm going to take a rope and tie it around my neck! Get out to the washstand and wash your head!"

The house has finally wound up stripped naked in the middle of the pasture, with not a tree near it but the Indian laurel tree that Grandma didn't let them cut down. The house is so ugly without any trees! It's so lopsided the walls are practically dragging on the ground. And I figure when hurricane season comes this house will never stand the first breeze. Then the house will fall in on top of us and we'll run out and get soaking wet and try to find a tree to get under, but since there aren't any trees anymore where will we go when the hurricane comes and blows the house down?

Celestino is crying out behind the thicket of wild pineapples. If Celestino takes it into his head to write poems on the leaves of these wild pineapple plants, Grandpa is sure to set fire to the whole thicket.

The thicket is blazing on all four sides, and a baby buzzard flew up and out of it with his wings on fire and fell on top of the house. The roof caught fire and now the whole house is blazing. The baby buzzard is burned to cinders and he falls right in the middle of the parlor . . .

"Our Father, Who art in heaven . . ."
Grandma drops to her knees and picks up the baby bird.
"Water! Water! Get water to put out the fire!"

My mother is the packhorse—she runs back and forth between the house and the well with buckets over her shoulders, full of water, and huffing and puffing and running as fast as she can.

Grandma gets down on her knees in the yard and lifts the baby buzzard up as high as she can, as high as her arms can reach. Then she starts dancing and jumping up and down and she runs off like a shot towards the Indian laurel tree. When she gets there she makes a big high jump and all of a sudden she changes into some kind of strange bird that screeches like a woman. The bird just sits real still on the very highest twig of the Indian laurel tree, and I start throwing rocks at it. But my aim is so terrible that all I manage to do is scare it away. So it flies off and disappears in the air, turning into just another one of those buzzards.

The fire is out. And Celestino is still crying, out behind the thicket of wild pineapple. Poor Celestino! I feel so sorry for him, and he does for me too.

I know he does for me even if he's never told me so. I know he's felt sorry for me ever since the day Grandpa picked me up by my throat and told me, "You son of a bitch, you by-blow— here you eat because I let you. So go bring in the calves if you don't want me to boot you and your mother both out of this house."

By-blow!

By-blow!

"Damned stubborn jackass calves. Today not a one shows up."

By-blow!

"You jackasses! Keep walking if you don't want me to break your legs!"

By-blow!

"You jackasses! Walk! . . ." The *son of a bitch* part doesn't bother me because I already know about that. But that *by-blow* part. What in the world does "by-blow" mean, I wonder.

"Mama, what does 'by-blow' mean?"
"Take your finger out of your mouth, ninny!"
"Mama. What . . ."
"I said take your finger out of your mouth, goddammit!"

I can feel this great huge sadness on my shoulders tonight and I don't know who to talk to about it. Oh, I know—I'll talk to Celestino about it . . . No, the poor thing has enough to worry about with his own problems.

So, so sad. I slipped in the pasture and broke my knee. I really did break it, I swear, and it bled like anything. The calves all ran off and got away, and one got lost way down below the river. When I told Grandpa about the lost calf, he didn't say a word to me—he just went off to the woods. He took the machete out of its scabbard and cut a long thin twig off a thistle plant. He peeled the twig real slow. He trimmed it real clean and nice. Then he swished it through the air and he said to me, "Come here."

I went.

"Stand there and keep still."

And I stood by him and kept very still. Then he started switching me. First on my back. Then on my neck. Then on my head and then on my face and then one two three four times on my hands.

I didn't say anything or cry, and that must have made him madder because he switched me twice, for extras, on the end of my nose, and I thought, "As long as he doesn't get me in the eyes I don't care." And he didn't get me in the eyes.

Then I guess he got tired. He threw the broken switch on the ground and went off to find the calf that had wandered off. I saw him getting farther away and first I was relieved and then I got as mad as a mad dog. So mad that I thought about pulling up a piece of fence paling and stabbing him in the back. I felt like doing that. But I didn't—Grandpa is so sly he would have guessed even what I was thinking if I'd pulled up the paling, and before you could blink it would be me, not him, that had a fence post stuck through my heart. "You'll pay for this," I said. And I started to cry from being so mad. And as I was crying I remembered that I still didn't have the slightest idea what "by-blow" meant.

The thicket of wild pineapples stopped burning. Across the ashes, where once in a while a brand or two still throws off sparks, comes Celestino with a stake through his heart.

"What have they done to you?"

I asked Celestino that as I tried to pull the stake out of his heart.

"Leave it there." He smiled at me. "Just leave it there, it'll come out of its own accord."

And he kept walking over the singed ground covered with smoldering pieces of plants and wood that sizzled and sparked like skyrockets. Uh-huh, like skyrockets, and in fact it was in the middle of all the New Year's celebrating. I tried to keep walking along beside Celestino, to see if I could convince him to let me pull the stake out. But *ha!* There was no way I could do that. My feet aren't made out of iron, to be able to walk along like it was nothing at all on top of a red-hot bed of coals. So I gave up on that idea. So then I was alone and the great huge sadness came again and made me feel butterflies in my stomach. "By-blow," said a lizard to me as he sizzled to a crisp, and he said it in a very nasty tone of voice, like he was making fun of me. I was going to give him a kick but my foot got roasted, almost, before I could get to him. So I limped all the rest of the way down to the river. My foot was burning like a live coal! If I could have I'd have cut it off. But on second thought—I'm almost down to the river now. If I hadn't already cried once, a little while ago,

I'd start crying again. All of a sudden I remember that for the very first time Celestino has spoken to me. Uh-huh, he spoke to me when I tried to pull the stake out of his heart! He spoke to me! He spoke to me!

And now that urge to bawl I had has gone away.

And it's almost morning. Morning again. And behind the clouds an almost-white glow begins to come out, so I can make out where the tree trunks are and keep from running into them. I start running and I can feel something like sleet coming down right in my face, making my face and eyes feel much much cooler.

"Hurry up with those buckets of water, child!"

"I'm coming! I'm coming!" With this sun so hot it's splitting rocks, and me carrying water like a mule.

"I said *move!* Are you listening to me!"

"Wait a minute. I've got to rest!"

"You're lazier than a stick! I don't know why lightning didn't strike me before I had a son like this!"

"I'm coming," I said—you'd think these buckets full of water didn't weigh a thing. And this is the fifth trip I've made to the river! That's right! To the *river,* because in the dry times the well doesn't have a drop of water. So now I'm the one who gets screwed with carrying water on a pole from the river to the house.

"Hurry up! The coleus is all shriveled up!"

"I'm coming! Can't you see I'm just resting!"

"Don't talk back to your mother! You spoiled wart!"

And I'm as bored as spit. All I ever do is carry water. Water so Grandpa can wash his dirty feet. So Grandma can rinse out her hank of hair—thank goodness Grandma washes her hair just once a month. But anyway, it's always *me* that has to carry the water. Carry water so my mother can take her baths and water the plants. Because she's gotten it into her head that all the plants in front of the house have to be watered, and she won't let up. I've got to break my back so she can even water the wormseed plants! This makes five trips, and there's still the barrel and the crocks for drinking water to go. And the worst part of it is that the crocks leak so I can never get them all the way full . . .

"Don't you ever plan to get here with that water!"

In the crock there's a frog . . .

"Child!"

There's always a frog in the water cabinet where the crocks are and I know for a fact that it's the same frog there every day. They say if you poke a frog with a stick, it will squirt milk in your eyes and you'll go blind. But that isn't true because I've poked and prodded that frog, and I've even shaken him in my hands, and I still see more than you'd give me credit for.

"Move with those buckets if you don't want me to take a fence paling to you!"

"I'm coming! I'm coming!" Ugh, these buckets are heavy. Let's see if I can lift this pole with both buckets on one end . . . Bang! There they go, both of them rolling off. Now my mother will put out my eyes like she was the frog herself.

"Now you've spilled the water! You get ready, because I'm going to fill up those buckets with the juice I get out of your hide! You get ready, you miserable child!"

To get away from the frog I've climbed way way up to the highest part of the Indian laurel tree. But the frog is right behind me and he yells at me, "Wait till I catch you—I'll get water out of your hide!" But I'm too high and I don't think he can hop all the way up here. But anyway I keep climbing up to the very very top. Now I'm in the highest, thinnest part of the tree. The frog has started hopping, slowly but surely, up the trunk of the tree.

"Wait till I catch you! I'm going to put out your eyes!"

This branch just barely holds me up, and if I fall down to the ground I'll burst like a watermelon, and if I climb down out of the tree the frog will put out my eyes.

"Wait till I catch you! I'll teach you to have a little respect for your mother! You spoiled wart!"

The frog has started swelling up and now he's great big huge. I don't know what to do now. The frog gives a hop and catches me by the throat.

"I'll put out your eyes!"

He opens his great big mouth and shoots some scalding-hot milk at me and my face starts frying and I go blind. I try to wiggle out of his sticky legs but we start falling towards the ground, all tangled up with each other.

I wish I knew where Celestino spent the night. Where he slept, if he slept at all. And if he's been able to pull the stake out of his heart. I hope he hasn't taken it into his head to go on writing poems on the trunks of the trees, because we're going to wind up living in the middle of the desert if he does.

I jump from tree trunk to tree trunk till I come to the house, and the first thing I see is the white roof through the fog and all my cousins up on top of it, yelling and screaming and singing silent songs that just they and I can understand. I hop into the rainspout and climb up on the roof. The chorus of cousins comes over to me, still jumping up and down, and all of them at once say to me,

"Why have you made us wait so long? You know perfectly well we disappear as soon as the sun comes out. How inconsiderate! This fog is the only thing that protects us from people. Is it that you don't want to kill your grandfather anymore?"

"No, I want to! I want to!"

"Then at least be on time to the meeting. You called it yourself."

"It's that Celestino is lost on the mountain and I've spent all night looking for him . . ."

"Bull! Celestino is asleep behind the coca plants and you've been off on a wild-goose chase. Just spent the night jumping from one tree trunk to another and howling like a dog that's lost his master . . ."

"Well, I never stopped thinking about him, anyway."

"Now is the time to save him."

"Tell me—please—when can I kill Grandpa?"

"When they can think that you weren't the one that killed him."

"When is that?"

"When there are a lot of people in the house."

"Like at the party at Christmas?"

"Like at the party at Christmas."

"So—I can't even get drunk on that one day?"

"Not that day. But every other day you'll be able to."

"What about my mother?"

"May God bring her to His glory."

"What about my grandmother?"

"Now, you'd better let your imagination be, because as soon as you stop dreaming and sleep more, they won't bother you anymore. Stop worrying. Or worry less—Celestino is the only one that's still alive and it's up to us to protect him. You're It—save him. But we'd better go before that damned sun melts us. What a shame the night's so short for us! Now you listen to what we told you—don't worry so much, stop dreaming up so much trouble, and sleep." Sleep. Sleep Slee

"Go to sleep!" said my mother, and she started rocking me in the rocking chair with the caved-in seat. Poor Mama! Always rocking me so I can sleep in peace. But she better not think four rocks with the rocking chair and I'm asleep! Not a chance! For *me* to go to sleep, you've got to sing me Pop Goes the Weasel and tell me three or four stories but not the same one always or the ones I've heard before. Other stories, different from those ones that Grandma always tells me.

> *Rockaby baby, in the treetop,*
> *When the wind blows . . .*

"No, not that one! I already know that one!"

"Around and round the mulberry bush, the monkey . . ."

"Not that one either! You've sung me that one a whole lot of times already."

"Once upon a time there were three ants that lived in a turtle shell . . ."

"No! Not that one! Not that one!"

"Smack that boy and he'll go to sleep! So big and such a brat! *I'll* tell you one—four smacks on your ass, that's what!"

"Carmelina's husband left her again and she set herself afire. My poor sister! May she rest in peace. All the men just used her. When we'd go to the fair they'd all back her into a dark corner, and then . . ."

"Carmelina! My daughter! Carmelina! The poor thing! May God forgive her! And now what's to become of the child!"
Poor child!
Poor child!

"Just imagine, there was nothing for us to do but bring him here and finish raising him ourselves."

"Such a bad time, too! I don't know what we're going to feed him with, the drought is so bad now. Ay! What'll we feed him with! What'll we feed him with!"

"We'll feed him on shit!"

"Don't talk that way. Like it or not, he's your grandson. Your daughter's own son."

"Daughter my foot! The poor thing, God bless her, was nothing but a whore. Such a whore! Ay, such a whore."

"Shut up!"

"And I don't even know what the child's name is. Poor creature!"

"Celestino! His name is Celestino! At least that's what the man that brought the news about Carmelina hanging herself told me, because she didn't just set herself afire; when she had the rope around her neck she took a bottle of alcohol and poured it all over herself. Poor thing! I just don't understand how a person could hang herself and set herself afire at the same time . . . That is really and truly peculiar. Isn't it just possible that somebody

I hope this letter finds you well.
I am fine. I am sending you a
can of Chinese luncheon meat.

Don't fail to eat it. It's the
very best quality . . .

—My mother

came along after she'd hanged herself and set her on fire just for spite? . . ."

"Celestino! Tell me if that's not the ugliest name they named the miserable creature!"

"Ay, poor Carmelina! I thought about hanging myself one day, too. But I kept putting it off and putting it off. The hanging. And look at me, still here! I've got so little willpower. No will-power at all! . . ."

"May God forgive you . . ."

"God can burn in hell for all I care!"

"My God. This is no daughter of mine, she's a she-ass!"

"Like mother like daughter."

"Rude!"

"Old she-goat!"

"You're the she-goat! And a lying *crazy* she-goat!"

"Our Father—my father—my mother has called me crazy again. Ay, she called me crazy . . ."

"Don't cry, silly, I'll see to your *mother.*"

"Tell me that story, Mama! Keep telling it! And you too, Grandma! Keep on, keep on, you too! That's the one I like!" Thank goodness they've finally told me something besides Pop Goes the Weasel. "Keep going! Keep going! . . ."

"You've wet the bed again! What do you think you are, a baby? You're too big for that! You better be sure your grandfather doesn't find out, or he'll give you a switching!"

"It's that I'm scared to go out into the yard at night to go to the outhouse."

"Scared of what?"

"Of the dead people. They say this place is full of dead people . . ."

"What a goose you are! . . . Help me get this mattress into the sun . . ."

The other night when I couldn't hold it, and it wouldn't have just been a *wet* bed either, I did go out, and I saw a white shape run behind the kitchen. I got so scared I didn't need to go to the privy anymore. And I told Grandma about it and she says that's the ghost of Old Lady Rosa that walks around dragging her chains because they don't weed her grave and also because they didn't say the novena when she died.

"Mama's gone crazy. That's her that goes out to go to the privy every night because she spends the livelong day eating all kinds of filth and garbage and as soon as she goes to bed her insides start churning and growling inside her . . . As though I didn't hear it every night! . . . Grab the mattress by that corner there! . . . What a smell! If you wet this bed again I'm going to tell your grandfather and he'll give you four good ones with a switch! We need to see how we can fix this bedroom—today Carmelina's son is coming, and he's going to sleep with you."

"There comes Carmelina's son."

"The poor thing has his hanged mother's face."

"Don't mention his mother to him . . ."

"Or his father either."

"Leave him alone, now."

"Give him a little milk and coffee and see if there's not a piece of boiled sweet potato left from lunch."

"Don't stuff him with filth, now, and make him spend all night trotting back and forth from the house to the privy like you do."

"Rude!"

"Stupid!"

"She-ass!"

"Mule!"

"She-ass!"

"Muuuullle!"

"God let you die!"

"God doesn't listen to wild animals!"

"Ingrate!"

"Old shitty-britches!"

.　　.　　.

"This is our bedroom."

"Smells like piss."

"At night ghosts come out here."

"In my house every night seven ghosts would come out, all different colors . . . Phew!"

"Grandma, yesterday he told me at his house every night seven all different-colored ghosts would come out . . ."

"Holy Virgin! What a load that poor creature has on his shoulders! . . ."

"Oh, and he also told me that you smelled like piss."

"Most Holy Virgin!"

"This Celestino is the *laziest* boy in the world. Not a thing I tell him to do gets done. And when I tell him, 'Mind your grandfather because he's the one that puts food in your mouth,' he starts scratching and digging in the ground and whistling like I was talking right through him. A nice load we get dumped on us!"

"Before we go to bed we better stop up the cracks because some dead person could slip through there."

"No. Leave them like that. My mother used to say it was better to leave the cracks open so air could come in."

"Grandma, he told me to leave the cracks open because his mother came every night as soon as the wind started blowing."

"Holy Virgin! We've got to see how we can get rid of that child."

"Your mother—why did she hang herself?"

"I don't know. But that afternoon two sweet potatoes she put on to roast burned up on her and that bothered her a whole lot and all day long she didn't say another word, and when I asked her what was wrong she told me to go to hell, and by early that night she was strung up from the Indian sumac tree . . ."

"Cover my head up too. I'm scared."

"I'm dripping with sweat . . ."

"If my mother hanged herself we could both tell the same stories."

"So cold!"

"I'm roasting."

"Why don't we hang *ourselves* too?"

"We will tomorrow."

"No, it's better to do it right now."

"No, I said tomorrow was better."

"Your face has water all over it."

"It's that I'm crying."

"That boy's not worth shooting—in the middle of the planting he drops the sack of corn and sits down and breaks out crying in the middle of the field! What a good-for-nothing!"

"If we could just get rid of that pig slop!"

"His mother—may God forgive her—was worthless too."

"What a hussy! To do that and leave her child to wander all over the face of the earth. I can't say I go along with that in the least! If we gave her her deserts we'd dig her up and tell her, 'You whoring bitch! How dare you kill yourself if you've got a son! You Jezebel!' "

"It's true—we don't even have the right to hang ourselves . . ."

"If she was going to do it she ought to have taken him with her."

"Hush, he's listening to us."

"He's started up that sniveling again."

"What a fate!"

"You don't know how to pray?"

"No."

"I don't either . . . Grandma always starts praying and she

goes right to sleep. But what can *we* do to get to sleep if we're not sleepy and we don't know how to pray?"

"Let's start counting turtles."

"We'd be better off counting blackbirds—they go faster."

"I'd like to go to the privy but I'm scared."

"Not me."

"Let's both of us go."

"Let's go."

Now we're in the middle of corn-weeding time. Celestino and I have made ourselves brothers—like in a story I heard once. We cut our fingers and traded a little blood. Except really, I pricked myself such a little bit that not a drop of blood came out. Celestino talks less and less every day, and with Grandma and Grandpa he doesn't even *mutter*. Grandma and Grandpa say he's like a cat, that closes his eyes when you feed him so as not to have to say thank you for it. But I don't believe that.

Celestino and I manage to work as little as possible, but as soon as Grandpa realizes we're dragging our feet, he comes over to where we are and gives us a switching. He always whips Celestino harder than me, and yesterday instead of hitting him with the switch he hit him with the hoe handle. Poor Celestino's eyes started watering. But he didn't cry.

I don't think this year's crop is going to come up very well at all. A big army of worms has gotten into the whole cornfield and the grass is practically choking it.

Grandma and Mama, and my aunt Adolfina with them, have started weeding. They didn't want to, but Grandpa made them. And they say, through their gritted teeth, that it's all the same to them whether the corn comes up or not or gives a single ear or not, and that they're used to going as hungry as a sow on a leash. But they still give the old man his due. Because when he gets really furious he doesn't care if it's at the mother that bore him. Take yesterday. When he went to drink his coffee he burned his mouth, because Grandma (and if you ask me she did it on purpose) gave it to him scalding hot; so he took the pot full of boiling coffee and made Grandma drink the whole thing right there, still steaming and all, without even coming up for air. Poor Grandma! I watch her weeding now and I tell myself, "I bet her guts are blistered."

There's a sun out today that splits rocks. It drains everything out of you. And Grandpa still won't give us his leave to go to the house. My mother has turned royal purple, because she never has been able to stand the sun—the blood goes to her head. It makes me so sad to see my mother working like a mule, and sometimes I wish I could help her.

"Mama, let me help you awhile with the hoe."

"Leave me alone if you don't want me to split your head open with it."

Mama is mean, so I heard somebody say last year at the party at Christmas. But I don't think so, I think (and I heard somebody say this at the party at Christmas too) that it's that she's bored with the world. Uh-huh, that's what I heard somebody say last year on Christmas Eve when Mama got so drunk she started jumping up and down and yelling. So my aunts, very straight-faced, they said it was a spirit and they took a flail of broomwood leaves and started flailing at her back. But, drunk and all, she told them to leave her alone, no spirit had got into her, and she didn't believe in any of that foolishness either. The only thing wrong with her, she said, was that she wanted to die. "All I want is to die," she said, and she rolled around on the floor. And I heard the rest of the people talking and whispering in the corners, saying, "Poor woman, she only had a husband for one night. Now *that* is sad."

"Weary of this world is what I'd say, and living with those parents of hers. A pair of savages."

FOR

WE CANNOT BUT

SPEAK THE THINGS

WHICH WE HAVE SEEN

AND HEARD.

—Acts 4:20

"She'd be better off dead."

"Don't say such things."

"And with a son not quite right. I mean the boy is not quite right."

"Mama, people say I'm not quite right."

"Don't pay any mind to those people. Go on, now. Go for water one more time, to fill up the crocks."

Since then I feel so, so sorry for Mama. I know she's basically a good woman, and on my birthday she always remembers to give me a kiss and all. That's why I almost never. get mad at her, because I know that woman that's always fighting is not my real mother. My mother is another one, always hiding inside the fighting one's skin, and all *she* does is smile at me and say, "Come over here and I'll·tell you the story of the Seven Sisters . . ."

I figure Grandpa forgot we had to eat lunch today, since the sun is already past the middle of the sky and it keeps going down and down and the old man hasn't even raised his eyes off the ground . . . Grandma I think is the maddest one of all of us. Grandma is so old and so skinny! She's as skinny as the stick to poke the cats with. I figure if she keeps it up another hour in this sun she won't be able to get out of bed for a month.

"Grandma, you want me to help you for a while?"

"Go do your own work and let me be!"

There's no way to understand that woman. Her tongue is hanging out, and when I ask her if she wants me to help her, she tells me to let her be . . . Well, I better keep working or Grandpa will give me another whipping. I've already had four! . . .

Now I know why Grandma doesn't want me to help her—
she's not cleaning anything, what she's doing is pulling up the
corn plants by the roots. Uh-huh, I just realized the trick. Grandma
pulls up the plant, breaks off the stalk, and pretends she's planting
it again. The plant stands straight up, and anybody would think
it was planted, but it's broken off underneath and two or three
days of sun will completely dry it out . . . Then she grabs the
grass around it and pulls it out and goes on to the next one. And
look how hard she's working! . . . Lord save Grandpa!, he doesn't
know what kind of crow's gotten into his field.

Celestino has stumbled over a rock and knocked down I don't
know how many corn plants. Grandpa sees what's happened and
comes running over to where Celestino is lying on the ground,
and he starts chopping at him with the hoe. He finally leaves
him alone and goes back to the furrow he was weeding. I get so
mad inside, but I don't dare say a word because Grandpa would
chop me into little pieces with the hoe too and I know that hurts
a whole lot. I know that hurts a whole lot even if Celestino didn't
make a peep and is standing there now staring down at the ground,
not even lifting his head once. Meanwhile the sun keeps growing
and growing and growing until it finally melts us. My mother
has turned into a great big corn plant, and we all start pulling off
her ears of corn and eating them. Every time I pull off an ear she
whimpers, and bawls, but very very soft. Raw corn is so good! I
love it. I pull a whole lot of ears off my mother so I can carry
them back and roast them in the cookstove. Grandpa has finished
planting Celestino and he tells me we can go now.

"Have we worked today!" I tell him, smiling and eating the
corn off the cob.

"A lot! A lot! But we've finally finished planting Celestino.
We'll see what kind of crop I get. I hope it rains!"

Singing, skipping and running, Grandpa and I leave the field.
We shake hands and throw rocks at the blackbirds. Skipping and
jumping up and down and laughing as hard as we can, while the
sun shines and shines and the corn plants sparkle and wink in

Do not ask her whence she comes.
Her history is of little account.
In their poverty,
her parents sold her for
a bag of white rice.

—THE MAGIC MIRROR

the midday glare. We go off like that, until the first big drops start dropping, hard. So then we take off running madly all the way across the field, until we come to the house, where Grandma, tied to the cookstove with a rope around her neck, has lunch already ready for us.

Celestino and I have escaped from the cornfield and come down to the river to swim. The river is almost completely dried up, and the only place where you can swim is in the black pond where all the cows go to drink. This water, so they say, is putrid. But if that was true all the cows would have died.

I'm the first one in the pond.

The water gets all stirred up and you have to be absolutely still for a while for it to settle so you can see the bottom again. Celestino is still taking off his clothes. Once the water is quiet I slip real real slow to the bottom of the river and, still swimming, I open my eyes. You see so many things in a riverbed with your eyes open! If you could just stay here forever. On the bottom of a river, swimming real real slow and going no place in particular, and with your eyes open . . . The rocks are white. So white that you'd hardly think they were rocks. And even the fish look different, and shinier. The bottom is a little dark, it's true, because there's hardly any sand and leaves cover the little there is, but I try to swim as slow as I can and to not scrape the bottom so it doesn't get stirred up. As long as I can hold my breath I'll stay under here and not stick my head out, like the turtles do . . . A bunch of little tiny sunfish go by, and they tickle my feet. Then they act like they get scared and swim off real fast. Then bream swim past in a line. Bream are so curious, they even sniff at my earlobes. They must be hungry. I blink at them real hard and they disappear, whoof!, but they come back and start bothering me again. I don't want to shoo them away because I know if I do the water will get all black and dirty, so black you wouldn't know whether you were at the bottom of a river or a loblolly like that one that Grandpa makes next to the washbasin at my house, where Celestino and I used to go swimming when they wouldn't let us come down to the river. Grandma would tell us that that water in the loblolly would kill anybody that got in it, but we'd dive and splash in it all the time and nothing ever happened to us. And one time we brought a little crawfish up from the creek and threw it in the loblolly, to raise it there. I fed that little crawfish every day. But it was dead in a week. Except I don't know, sometimes I think it was Grandma that killed it because she always takes the other side, no matter what. And anytime she can do something mean to us, she'll do it. So then the loblolly got this terrible stink with the dead crawfish in it and for a week we didn't have any place to go swimming. Until one day we sneaked off and came down to the river. And since then we come every chance we get . . . A great big huge crawfish just went by underneath me, with Grandma in its claws. What pretty colors on that crawfish! My grandmother's not squirming or struggling, and the crawfish starts swallowing her, little by little, but then the rest of the crawfish come over and grab Grandma away from the first one. And then they all start squabbling and fighting. But finally they chomp her up. A bunch of crawfish look over at me, like they just saw me, and they say, "Him, him, he's in the family too." I try to get to the top of the water before they chomp me up. But they grab me. They pull at me, and then they start eating me up alive . . . Celestino has jumped in the pond. The water gets all black and the two of us swim over to the bank.

"What a muddy mess!"
"We better wait till it settles."
"Meanwhile, I'm going to go to sleep."
"Me too."

We've come to the river. On the way I discovered a kingbird nest. I climbed up the tree where the nest was and it had four baby kingbirds. Celestino didn't want me to take the baby birds. But I told him we'd take just one of them and we'd raise it like our own child. So he said that was all right then, to take just one and leave the rest of them for their parents, so their parents could live with the loss and not die of sadness. Sadness! Whoever heard of birds dying of sadness!, I said, and laughed. So he told me not to laugh because that just showed how much I knew. And he looked very very serious.

So with the baby bird cheeping and fluttering we came to the house.

"Let that bird loose!" my mother told me when she saw me come into the house carrying the baby kingbird.

"No! Celestino and I are going to raise it like our own child."

"That's all we needed!" she answered. But then she looked real real serious too, and she didn't open her mouth again that whole day and night.

We went out to find some persimmons and seeds and things for the baby bird.

Today is the last day of weeding in the cornfield. Thank goodness, because I don't think I could take another day of it. "If this keeps up," I tell Celestino, very very soft so nobody can hear me, "I'm hiding under the bed and not ever coming out again." He doesn't pay me any mind, he just goes on weeding and pulling out clumps of grass . . . Grandma is the busiest one of all of us— pulling up and then replanting the corn plants, except without any roots now. Just wait till Grandpa catches her. I'd hate to see it—the day he catches her at it, he'll kill her. As soon as we're through here, Celestino and I are going to go up to the mountain to cut down a crepe myrtle bush and make the baby kingbird a cage. He's already getting feathers. Poor thing, we take the best care of him we can, and I even lay him down in the bed some- times, but I don't know, it looks to me like he hardly ever eats. So that's why I stuff him. I take a little bit of persimmon and I put it in his mouth and I roll it down his throat right to his gullet, with my finger.

"You goddamned she-ass! So you're pulling up the plants! You just wait, I'm going to cut off your head! Goddamned old biddy! Whore! Heathen savage! Today's the day I'm finally going to kill you!"

I knew that was going to happen. Grandma thinks she's such a sharp one, but I'll tell you for a fact she's a goose . . . There she goes, running as fast as she can go. And Grandpa after her, almost reaching her. If he catches her he'll bury the hoe in her head and split it right down the middle, like it was a half-ripe coconut. Grandma has hotfooted it into the house yelling like a banshee and bolted all the doors. Celestino and I just stand there with our mouths half open in the middle of the cornfield, and Mama and my aunt Adolfina take off running behind my grandfather. People going along the road don't even stop to see what's going on—everybody in this part of the country knows us by now, so they know what kind of people we are. Nobody even talks to me, and I'm still little. Wait till I grow up! and then they'll play tricks and practical jokes on me, like they're always playing tricks on Grandpa, and they'll cut my fences so the neighbors' stock will come onto my place and eat everything I've planted, which is another thing they do to Grandpa. But a lot of it is his own fault. If people treat us like that it's because he's such an old curmudgeon—if he was nicer to people these things wouldn't happen to him. But he's as stupid as anybody could ever be, and one time he beat one of Baudilio's cows to death with a fence post because she was trying to get into the garden. Baudilio came over later that day so mad he was practically frothing at the mouth, to settle scores with Grandpa. But Grandpa grabbed him by the scruff of the neck, and if Baudilio's wife hadn't shown up at that very instant and started screaming, her husband would have been dead as a doornail . . . What a squawk Grandma's making! What a racket! She sounds like a hen that doesn't want the rooster to mount her but the rooster sneaks up behind her and grabs her when she's not looking! . . . The only person that's scared of what will happen is Celestino, and it's that he's not used to this kind of thing yet. I don't get scared anymore; in fact, it's almost fun—and Mama doesn't get scared anymore either, since she's so used to arguing and fighting that if a day were to go by without some kind of a row, she'd feel a little let-down. And I figure if she picked up the fence post she picked up it was to whack Grandma, not Grandpa, with it, or maybe to whack both of them. Because she doesn't know who to hate the most. But if you ask me, I think in this particular set-to Mama's whack is for the old woman.

Grandpa has been trying to kick the door down, but since he can't kick it open or break it down, he climbs up on top of the roof and jumps inside through the hole I made in the palm thatch. So then Grandma shoots outside like an arrow, through the parlor door, and she's still bawling and bellowing as she heads for Baudilio's house, where I figure she'll ask for some help. We just watch the figures of Grandpa with the hoe over his shoulder, my mother waving the fence post around, and Adolfina with her sewing scissors bringing up the rear.

One after the other they disappear in the direction Grandma already disappeared in. So from where we're still standing Celestino and I can't hear anything but Grandma yelling or see anything but the cloud of dust she left behind.

The baby kingbird is dying on us. I know he's dying on us.

I gave him water, but it didn't help. I gave him nice ripe persimmons, but it didn't help. I gave him bread sopped in milk, but it didn't help. He's dying on us.

Now I fix up a little box guava candy came in to bury the baby bird. But he's still alive . . . He's dying on us! But he's still alive!

How sad! Oh, I hope the baby bird doesn't see me making the coffin for him, I hope he doesn't see that even while he's still alive we're thinking about when he dies. But you have to think about those things, because if we left him in the cage he'd rot and the ants would come and eat him.

"The coffin is made."
"He's still alive."
"Don't cry, he's still alive."
"Alive."
"Don't bawl."
"Don't bawl."

.   .   .

He's dying. I can see him shivering in one of the corners of the cage, and I know he's dying of sadness. And to think I thought birds couldn't be sad! . . . Well they can!, because if he wasn't sad what else would he be dying from? I gave him milk, I gave him water, I put his cage in the sun, I laid him in the bed, I ran my hand over him, I prayed an Our Father for him, I set him close to the cookstove, I made a sign of the cross over him, I gave him some persimmons, I helped the food down his gullet, I rubbed his feet, and then I wanted to give him a laxative but I didn't because according to my grandmother that was a damn-fool thing to do.

"Whoever heard of a kingbird taking a laxative? Let him die in peace—it's all your own fault anyway for taking him out of the nest!"

"What can I do for him before he dies? Is there anything I can do for him? . . ."

"Just let him die in peace."

I've given him cold water, so now I'll give him hot water. What can I do for him! . . . I'll cross myself for him again, and make one over him too—Our Father which art in heaven hallowed which art in heaven hallowed which art in heaven hallowed which . . . I wonder what the next word is after that. I don't know how to pray anymore. But—well—anyway. I'll move my lips like almost everybody that doesn't know how to pray does when they make themselves out to be holy. I'll move my lips. Let him be saved!

"Mmmmmmmmmmmmmmmmmmmmmmmmmmmmmmm mmmm mmmmmmmmmmmmmmmmmmmmmm mmmmm mmmmmm m m mmmmmmmmmmmmm m mm mmmm mm mmmmmmmmmmmmmmmm" I better keep moving my lips until the time a prayer would last has gone by. But how long does a prayer last? Well, I'll keep moving them a little while longer yet, just in case MMMMMmm mmmmmmmmmmmm mmmmmmmmmmmm mmmmmmmmmmmmmmmmmmmm mmm mmmmmmmm . . .

54

"Celestino! Celestino! How long does a prayer last?"

"Mmmmmm   mm m mmmmmmmmm m   mmmm."

"Mmmmm   mmmmmmmm   mmmmmm m."

"Mmmmmmmmmm."

"Mmmmmmmmmmmmmmmmmm."

"MMMMM MMMM MMmmmmmmmmmm . . ."

"Leave him alone! Let him rest in peace."

He's dying! . . . mmmmmmmmmmmmmmmmmmmmmmm
mmmmm . . . But how long does a prayer last? Mmmmmmmm
mmmmmmmmmmmmmmmm. We'll count to a hundred.
We'll count to a thousand. Do you know how to count? I can
count to ten, but that's all I know how. Count! Count! Mmmm
mmm . . . One two three four five six seven eight . . . Mmmmm
mm mmmmmmm mm mmmmmmmmmmmmm mmmm
mmm mm mmmmmmm mmmmm . . . Such a pretty day! said
my mother, and she set me astraddle her waist and started walking all over the field full of just-blooming marigolds.

"Who plants these marigolds, Mama?"

"Nobody. They grow all by themselves."

"All by themselves! . . . To think they're so pretty and they
grow all by themselves. Who waters them?"

"Nobody. Nobody waters them. They must get enough water
from the rain."

Then Mama got down on the ground and the two of us started
pulling up marigolds, until there were too many to hold anymore
so we started making a mountain of marigolds. The mountain
was so big that it reached all the way to the sky and broke a hole
in it . . .

"Celestino! Celestino! The baby kingbird is dead now! . . ."

And through the hole my mother disappeared. I called her.
But the hole closed up again. So I was all by myself in the middle
of the field full of marigolds, that smelled so strong that I opened
and shut my nose to play with the smells and make myself realize

how nice the perfume was. My mother didn't come back, no matter how much I called her. I even looked under the rocks, but the only thing I could find was a chorus of scorpions that told me, "She's not here." "She's not here." So I kept picking up rocks and looking under them, and a chorus of crickets told me the same thing—"She's not here." I finally gave up and started back to the house. And on the way back I remembered I'd gone to the mountain in the first place to get some marigolds to put on the dead baby kingbird. But when I looked back all I saw was my mother, carrying a switch, running after me and coming up to me and telling me, "Either you go get the water or I'll see to it you don't set foot in the house again today. Ever since that good-for-nothing Celestino came you've spent every waking minute running around doing nothing and you haven't carried a single bucket of water. But the fun is over—you either bring water or you don't sleep in the house! Do you hear me?"

"Shit! I'm not carrying anything—not today I'm not!" I told her. I was fighting mad, but that wasn't what I really wanted to tell her. I wish I could have said, "Don't you see the little baby kingbird we were taking care of has died? I just don't feel like doing anything today." That's what I wish I had told her. But I didn't, because I know if I'd told her she would have burst out laughing. Burst out laughing.

So I took off running all through the pasture, my mother yelling curses after me and screaming, "You don't set foot in this house today! Don't think you will! Today you're going to have to sleep in the pasture! Like the cows!"

But that's not the way it turned out. After it got dark and we could bury the baby kingbird and put a handful or two of bluebells on top, Celestino and I slipped across the roof, slid down the gutters the rainwater runs down when there are rainstorms, and waited there, real real patiently, huddled up against each other until Mama started snoring. And when she gave out the first hwonk, we skipped right into the bedroom. And we ran and got into bed, trying to breathe as quiet as we could. We were laughing ourselves to death and holding it back too, and finally we went to sleep.

·　·　·

GREAT

TOOTHED

FORNIVORES !

— My crazy uncle
Faustino

The first claps of thunder woke us up. This is August, and it always rains, except I don't understand why so early. A big huge bolt of lightning hits us and I jump straight up in the bed. Celestino gives another jump, too, and I can't keep from breaking out laughing, so I laugh as hard as I can. But since there's one clap of thunder after another after another, he can't even hear me. Thank goodness! because if he heard me laughing at him he might get mad at me, except that's pretty hard, because he's never gotten mad in his whole life. Or sad, or happy, or anything. I'd never thought about that, but now I realize that Celestino is always the same—mad, sad, happy, and everything all at the same time. I don't know how he manages to always have the same expression. I can't be that way—when I feel bad I have to do something, even if it's just kill a lizard, and when I'm happy I start dancing and hopping up and down. Except sometimes I dance and jump up and down without feeling one bit happy. It's awfully hard to understand that. But Celestino is even harder to understand.

"You never cry?"
"Why do you ask me?"
"Because I never see you cry."
"What do *you* know . . ."
Now the rain has gotten worse. It's morning, but everything is pitch dark. Big hard raindrops are falling, almost in rhythm, and dripping through the roof and dripping on us, between the sheets. I jump straight up and then get out of bed, but the floor is like a lake. So I get back into bed. Everything is darker now, and the only thing I can see is Celestino's face when a quick flash of lightning leaks in through the chinks in the wall. The rain keeps getting worse, and a big flock of swallows flutter and fly out of the branches of the Indian laurel tree, and it looks like they just dissolve in the rain.

"Look at the swallows! Look at the swallows! They can get out in the middle of a rainstorm and go wherever they feel like . . ."
"What do *you* know . . ."

. . .

Another flash of lightning. Now I can really see Celestino's face. Except with all the racket of the thunder and rain I didn't hear what he said to me when I showed him the swallows . . . I love rainstorms. Every time after it clears off, Celestino and I go up to the mountain, hopping from one puddle to the next, and swim in the first little pool we come to. The water is so clear and cold after a rainstorm! And all the birds! There are so many birds! Cheeping and singing so much that I have to yell at Celestino for him to hear me . . . Now some skinny little tiny flashes of lightning are striking. They look like glowing firebrands somebody's throwing up in the air out behind the house. After every lightning flash there comes a big huge crack of thunder and then another lightning flash. If I could get out of bed I'd go out into the breezeway and watch the rain come down (because I've made up every bit of what I just told—I haven't seen a thing), but we can't. A skinny lightning bolt came into the room a minute ago and told us, "Just keep still unless you want me to sizzle you." So here we are, still as we can be. I look at Celestino and Celestino looks at me, except we can't see each other. Maybe at this very moment he's crying. And I can't see him! Maybe I'm crying too. But I don't think so. As dark as it is, I don't like to cry, because nobody could see me.

The door of the bedroom flies wide open and my mother, who's almost turned into a fish, comes in.

"My poor babies," she says to us. "You've spent this whole terrible storm in here all by yourselves. You must be frozen. I'd better lie down with you and warm you up, like the hens do with their little chicks when they first come out of the eggs."

My mother jumps into the bed and lies down with us. And in a little while we're colder than we were before, because my mother is as cold as a hailstone. So we pull the sheet up over our heads, but we're still numb from the cold.

"I can't," says the fish that had lain down in the bed with us. And it gives a deep deep sigh, that sounds almost like a scream to me, jumps out of bed, and swims off under the water.

Celestino and I stay under the sheet. We don't dare move, and we're shivering with cold. Now everything is soaking wet, including us. Is there no sign at all that the sky might be clearing off? Can that be? By now the bed is floating on top of the water. And Celestino and I are sailing all over the bedroom, not knowing where to make harbor. The door flies open again and my mother comes in like a streak, carrying the strap.

"Aha! So you had the gall to come sleep in this house! I told you you were going to sleep in the pasture tonight!"

Mama comes over to me waving the strap and starts smacking me with it.

"You miserable child! Miserable child!"

And since she's such a goose every smack of the strap lands on poor Celestino's back, but none of this is his fault. He doesn't even whimper, so then, seeing that he doesn't say a word, I stick my head out from under the sheets and I say to Mama, "You goose! You're strapping Celestino, not me."

Mama gets even madder at that.

"You little oaf! Damn you!"

And she keeps hitting Celestino. I don't know what to say to her now. I try to take the strap away from her, but she's as strong as an ox and she doesn't let it go that easy. So I throw myself on top of Celestino and let the strap crack across *my* back.

"Let's get out of here!" Celestino says to me then. "Let's run away!"

So we jump out of bed into the stinking water and we escape out the chinks in the wall. Once we're outside in the yard we run to the Indian laurel tree and then on out to the woods behind it, while the lightning bolt that warned us not to get out of bed starts chasing us full steam, wrinkling up and stretching out through the middle of the rainstorm like a big boa constrictor made out of lights, and yelling at us—

"Get back in your bedroom or I'll sizzle you!"

But we don't go back. We keep running and running and running. And now the screams of my mother standing in the rainstorm fade into the constant lightning and the never-ending rumble and racket of the thunder.

It finally looks like it's going to clear off.

Celestino and I are huddled together inside a hollow Santa Maria tree trunk. We watch the sky getting bluer and bluer, the clouds running across in front of us, until they melt, down below the river. If we came out of this hole now, the first brightness of the day might very well melt us. No, we'd better stay here a little while longer, and wait to see what happens.

We're hungry. Celestino hasn't said a word to me since we left the house, but all the same I know he's hungry too. And sometimes (even if he tries to stop it) you can hear his stomach growling. What will there be to eat now that everything's all muddy! You can hear the river roaring down below there. The river never gets tired, and little by little it has dragged off almost all the land, and the trees, and now we're all that's left—here inside a hollow Santa Maria tree, surrounded by that boiling rush of blood-colored water that keeps growing and growing, and never stopping, and carrying off cattle, trees, and people—everything in one big huge rolling boiling rush of water swelling and roiling faster and faster, tearing down the vines that had still been hanging practically in thin air, and the occasional tree that had still been miraculously standing, heaven only knows how . . . Celestino is shivering behind the dripping, sap-leaking Santa Maria tree, with cockroaches all over its trunk. I see him trembling now. The flashes of lightning haven't stopped making our life difficult, even if it *has* stopped raining. This tree trunk is huge. The only light that comes in comes from the lightning bolts outside there, that light us up for a second and then leave us in the dark again. If I leave this hollow tree, I wonder, will somebody be waiting for me with a big spear, standing right in the middle of the door? If I get the nerve to come out, I wonder, will anybody be there to hold back my grandfather's hatchet, all filed and sharpened and shiny and saying Come on out? I wonder if somebody will grab me if I start breathing again. If we breathe, you want to bet we won't be found out? It's daytime now, but in this hole in a tree, full of big fat cockroaches, everything is still dark.

"Why don't we go outside?" I say to Celestino, after years and years and years. "We might as well, because they're not going to go away or ever leave us alone. And we can't stay here. We'll starve to death. Let's get it over with, right now."

. . .

I just swallowed the last cockroach in one gulp. I offered a piece of it to Celestino, but he told me no, he was full. So I grabbed it still alive and kicking, and I just popped it in my mouth. And I swallowed it in one gulp. Cockroaches don't taste so bad. At least that last one seemed to taste pretty good. But I'll bet that's why—because it was the last one. And now we know, we know there's no way out. I see my mother's spear glint through the crack in the hole now and then, and I wonder, "Who in the world gave that spear to my mother?" And the head of Grandpa's hatchet, shining and shining almost like the sun, and as hateful as ever.

"What do we do now? We've run out of cockroaches," I ask Celestino, so he cuts off one of his fingers and hands it to me. "You're too kind," I tell him, "but this won't solve anything." So he pulls off one of his arms.

I scream.

I scream, but not too loud. And as soon as I scream, I clap my hand over my mouth. I look at him for just a second, and then I run out of the hole. The glare stops me. Grandpa's hatchet makes my eyes tickle and then I feel the skin on my neck start creeping. You can still see flashes of lightning, way way off, so far away that you'd swear they weren't flashes of lightning but the lights from some sea city instead. But all of us know very well there's no ocean around here. Much less a city. We're all alone. I don't like to live so far away from people, because you spend your whole life long seeing visions. And the worst part of *that* is that you can never tell whether they're visions or not for sure, because there's not another soul in the whole place to ask. So we're the only ones to see them. A while ago I came out of my room to go to the privy and halfway there I bumped into a giant spider with the head of a woman, and it was crying like its heart was breaking. I was so scared when I saw it, but when I saw it was crying I said to myself, "It's a person." So little by little I went a little closer.

"What do you want?" I said, hardly shaking at all.

And waving all its legs around, it said to me, "I want you to kill my children! For over a week now they've been on my back and they're eating right through to my insides."

I looked up on the hump of the spider with a woman's head,

and sure enough I could see a whole lot of all different-sized little spiders moving around. It looked like an anthill. They were sticking their sharp legs, *mean*, into their mother's back, and she was crying and crying, but there was nothing she could do about it. "Come have something to eat," the little baby spiders told me, and they kept on digging and scrabbling around with their legs. And since all of a sudden I actually felt like climbing up there on top of the spider and starting to eat, the only thing I could do to save myself was run back to the house and jump into bed and forget about going to the privy, which was all right because the feeling that I wanted to go to the bathroom had gone away. But the problem is that the only person that saw the spider with the head of a woman is me. So nobody wants to believe me, and when I told Mama about it she told me I was crazier than my grandmother. And Grandma crossed herself when I told her about it and then she got down on her knees in front of the cookstove and said to me, "You're hexed." And Grandpa laughed in my face and answered me by saying, "You ninny! You fool! You're just like your grandmother, seeing ghosts everywhere! Go out and bring in the calves this minute—it's already late and we haven't even started the milking!" The only person that believed even one word of what I said was Celestino and I told him about it as soon as I got back into bed. He answered me, halfway between being asleep and awake, "The spider again. Don't waste your time worrying about her, she did the same thing when she was little." And he finished going to sleep. I didn't know what to think—he'd said "again," and this was the first time I'd ever seen her and ever told him about it. Suppose he'd seen her before? But then why hadn't he told me? We always told each other all about the things we did when we were by ourselves, and that was very little, too, because now we were always together . . . Now for sure there's no way out for me—my mother's spear runs and slips in the strangest kind of prickly, hot tickle. My grandfather raises the hatchet as high as he can, holding it in both hands, and takes careful aim—"right in the middle of his head" looks like what he's thinking—and his eyes gleam like a cat's when everything is dark. My grandmother, standing stiff and straight, just stands there, sort of juggling another hatchet between her two hands and testing the edge with her finger. She is a hateful hateful woman, and besides that she's a coward, and that's why she'll wait till my mother's spear is sticking out of my guts and my grandfather's hatchet has made two drinking gourds out of my skull, and then she'll give the final stroke—so then she'll be able to say that none of it was her fault. Old chicken, I say, with my mouth shut tight, I bet you don't dare be the first one to whack me with the hatchet! *Finally the singing underneath the sharp white dogs'-teeth stones begins, the buckets of water in the yard, ants with wings.* Grandpa's hatchet gleams, so I start crying softly, softly, so nobody will get scared (not me either). But I know I'm crying, all the same, so it doesn't matter whether I cry soft or loud; when all's said and done, I'm a chicken too. Such a little chicken, just like my grandmother, and I think, well, as long as I'm going to cry, and everybody knows it, I might as well do it right. So I start bellowing out loud, so loud that the sky goes Crrrrack and cracks into four pieces . . . That was when we saw Celestino for the first time, down there, under the tall tall almond trees in the woods, writing and writing and writing on the tree trunks and on the branches of all the trees, writing the longest one of all his poems. I saw him, and I stopped crying, except I don't know why, because I didn't even know if what he was doing with his knife was scribbling poetry or what. And I'll never understand how it could be that at that very instant Mama, Grandpa, and Grandma all realized what it was, like *that*, because they're just as ignorant as I am, or maybe more so, and none of them so much as knows how to draw a circle for an O. But be that as it may, all of a sudden they acted like I'd ceased to exist, and without so much as scratching me, they took off like a flash and started attacking Celestino, saying words to him so mean, so mean, that not even Grandpa when he starts in after the mare and she won't let him catch her had ever said the like before. Celestino saw them coming with the hatchets and the spear but he didn't make the least effort to run away. The big ninny, he just stood there, tears running down his face, trying to explain, "Let me finish, there's just a little more . . ." Then I never found out what happened because a whole lot of fire ants were eating my feet, and I got so mad that I ran off down to the river and jumped in headfirst so the miserable dirty ants would drown. But it turned out that that day they didn't do anything to Celestino, but he still hasn't finished writing that poem. He walks around, poor thing, like a lost soul—stealing knives and making one tree after another dry up, and then Grandpa comes along and chops them down. I feel so bad about the trees, especially about the crepe myrtles, because they get so pretty when January comes. My mother used to tell me that the reason the crepe myrtles get all covered with flowers was for the Three Wise Men, and they cover the ground with flowers so the Three Wise Men won't realize there's no snow here, just mud. Because, she says, if the Three Wise Men ever figure out that there's no snow around here, they'll never ever come back again. And that just might be true, too, because ever since the crepe myrtles started drying up, the Three Wise Men have forgotten about me completely, and the year before last they didn't bring me so much as the flashlight, let alone the batteries, I asked for at the top of my lungs and that like an idiot I left their camels all that grass for. Uh-huh, it's true—it makes me feel so bad to see how all the trees are drying up, and it makes me so sad to see Grandpa chop them down with one whack—even a mango or a poisonwood tree. It makes me so sad, but what can I do . . . Hatchets hatchets hatchets hatchets hatchets hatchets hatchets hatchets hatchets hatchets hatchets hatchets hatchets hatchets hatchets hatchets hatchets

"How do hatchets go?"
"They go *shhhhp*, like spirits mewling through the air."

"How do hatchets go?"
"They go *shhhhp . . . Shhhhp.*"

Hatchets and the sound of hatchets is the only thing you can see or hear in this hatchet house, wallpapered in hatchets and stuffed and slipcovered in hatchets, with hatchets hanging from the ceiling and from the palm boards and even from the ridgepole. The floor and the breezeway and the drainpipes are all made out of them. And even the fence posts Grandpa used to make a table to lay hatchets on are made out of hatchets. Hatchets. Hatchets. And Celestino writing like a madman even on the tiny tiniest branches of the thistle bushes.

Hatchets . . . And with one whack the trees go Cr-cr-creeeak and fall over, because that blasted old man has gotten so strong and his aim has gotten so good lately that it's terrible to see, and the other day I saw him pick up a hatchet out in the field, take aim with it two or three times in the air, and throw it as hard as he could, and it went straight for the soursop tree and chopped it to kindling. And Grandma, who thinks it's a sign every time a horse whinnies, ran out of the kitchen saying curse words, because she says that tree was holy, and now a curse is going to fall on us. And a lightning bolt hit us.

Hatchets . . . And now the lightning has camped right in the house, and it calls us all every name in the book. And it even tells us what we're going to die of.

Hatchets. Hatchets . . . And I am so afraid that one of these days Celestino will get the idea of doing that henscratching on his own body.

Hatchets. Hatchets.
If there's no racket from the hatchets I can't sleep. Hatchets . . .

"Hear that noise from Grandpa's hatchets?"
"Uh-huh, I hear it."
"Do you still have a long way to go to finish writing that poem?"

"Uh-huh."

"A long long long way?"

"A *long* way. I haven't even started yet."

Hatchets.

Hatchets.

Hatchets.

If there's no racket from the hatchets I can't sleep. Don't let it stop!

Don't let it stop!

Don't let it stop!

Hatchets hatchets hatchets . . . "What a pretty flashlight," all the boys told me. The Three Wise Men brought it to me, on their camels, I told them, and they all broke into a fit of laughing. Hatchets. Hatchets . . . What are they all laughing about? . . . Hatchets hatchets hatchets hatchets hatchets.

"What are you laughing about?"

"Hatchets! Hatchets! Who told you it was the Three Wise Men, you big ninny?"

"I saw them myself. Nobody told me—I saw them myself with my own eyes."

"Ha! ha! ha! It's not a real flashlight. Here—I bet you can't make my face light up."

So I raised the flashlight and lit up the boys' faces.

"What have you done!"

"Hatchets. Hatchets," I said, dying laughing. And I went into my room, where everybody was waiting for me. And I raised the flashlight and I lit up everybody's face.

·   ·   ·

Who would affirm that
    the light and the shadow
    do not speak ?

Only those who
    do not understand
    the language
    of the day and the night.

— Moussa - Ag - Amastan

You went to STEAL
some food,

but your grandfather
SAW YOU

and gave you

A WHACK WITH
THE BROOM.

— My aunt Celia

"My snakes and serpents! Arise, and call thyselves snakes and serpents!"

And everybody arose and called themselves snakes and serpents. And I almost died laughing again ... Hatchets. Hatchets ... And finally the flashlight gave a jump and lit up my grandfather's face over there, under the big bay trees (where one time I made a nest all by myself for the wild doves). He was giving the biggest whack I ever saw anybody give a tree in my life. All the bay trees started making these deep hoarse yells, and then they started moaning, and some of them meowing, and some whinnying, and then finally cheeping, cheeping, cheeping, like the little baby wild doves that by now were fa-a-a-l-l-i-in-g. Sideways. Slowly. Branch and all. I started to go hold up the trees, but I figured if I did the tree trunks would squash me when they fell over on top of me. "Don't chop them down. There's a dove's nest, with little baby doves and everything, up there." ... Hatchets hatchets hatchets. And the trees started meowing again. And then Grandpa gave *me* a whack, but I didn't meow or anything. Not a peep. I just lay there stock-still, lying on the ground and across the chopped-down tree trunks, and I saw an ant eating an orange rind, with the mud still stuck to it and everything. Then I closed my eyes and started to see the ant pick me up with his legs and carry me off to his house, way down under the hole in the privy, where the stink never even gets to.   Here.

"Are you asleep?"
"No. Not yet."
"It must be late."
"It must be late."
"Do you hear the racket of the hatchets now?"
"I certainly do."
"I'm scared tonight."
"Me too."
"A lot?"
"More than you are."
"Do you still have a long way to go to finish the poetry?"
"Do I!"

"How long?"

"I haven't even started yet."

"Cover my head with the sheet."

"It's covered up already."

When it stops raining we'll go and get fish out of the mud puddles again! The fish from mud puddles are so delicious! Every time Grandma sees us coming with them, she starts throwing a fit, and she says to us, "Throw that garbage out, it tastes putrid." But we don't, and since she won't let us cook them in the cookstove, we go off to the mountain. And there, on the other side of the river, we start cooking up the fish. Celestino brings three great big rocks and I go out to look for dry firewood. Then we put the fish on the fire and we watch them cook, until they get good and red and we can eat them. Sometimes we leave them to cook while we go for a swim in the river.

"There's barely a tree left standing. What are we going to do now? The sun is burning us up and you can't write any more poetry anymore."

"Don't worry. I've planted a whole lot of trees and they'll be big pretty soon."

"Should I turn out the light?"

"Uh-huh, but turn it on first."

Today we get to the river earlier than ever. It's still early in the morning, and you can hear the frogs croaking back and forth to each other as clear as can be. Once in a while a cricket goes *zzeeee* and then goes quiet again. Last night I tried to catch a cricket. I got out of bed, but no matter how hard I looked for him I couldn't find him, and the blasted thing kept scraping and scraping and scraping. As soon as I covered my head up and started falling asleep, the cricket started chirping again, right in my ears, louder than ever, and I got so upset I sat up in the bed and spent the whole night awake. Except he never made another peep. So now I don't care whether he chirps or scrapes or not. He can chirp till his throat is raw as far as I'm concerned . . . It's been days since Celestino wrote anything on the tree trunks. It's so strange. Everybody in the house is on tenterhooks, waiting to see what's going to happen. But none of us dares to say anything. This whole part of the country knows by now that Celestino writes poetry, in spite of the fact that we live way way far from anybody else. And nobody says hello to Grandma or Grandpa or to anybody else in this house anymore. It's been no telling how long since anybody said hello to my mother—ever since my father (and I don't know so much as who he is) brought her back one day and stood in the middle of the road and yelled at Grandpa at the top of his lungs and said, "I'm leaving this piece of bone and gristle here for you." And walked away like nothing had happened. He never even looked back. From that time on nobody in this whole part of the country so much as nods to my mother, because they say that when a man throws his wife out it's because she did something terrible. But I know my mother never did the least bit of anything terrible. And if my father brought her back to Grandpa's house it was because—and there's no doubt in my mind about this—he just wanted to lay down his burden and walk his road by himself . . . Grandma and Grandpa have taken such a hate to Celestino they can't bear to see his face, and now with this poetry it's even worse. My mother doesn't know which way to turn, but then she's starting to hate Celestino too because I pay more attention to him than I do to her, and now I don't even help her water the flowers like at least I did before. But one thing's for sure—I'm the one that has to carry all the water for her to waste however she wants, even watering the nettles. And my aunt Adolfina—the only thing she's good for is squabbling and fighting and painting her face and arms with white dirt and lemon . . . The problem is that the only person on Celestino's side is me. Me, who's got no say in anything. Me, who can't do a thing for him in this house. And a lot of the time when I do try to do something nice for him I'm so stupid and clumsy that all I do is trip over my own feet in a manner of speaking, and everything comes out even worse. But what counts is that I'm on his side and he knows it and that makes him so happy. It makes both of us so happy.

We get to the house as it's turning dark. My mother is out in the yard, with the flowers, waiting for me to bring her the water so she can water them.

"The coleus have completely dried out," she says, and looks straight at Celestino, like it was all his fault.

"Don't worry, we'll give them some water and you'll see, they'll come back like *that*," I say, and I go into the kitchen to get the pole and the buckets.

Celestino always wants to help me get the water, but I tell him no, let me do it, because if Mama sees me with him carrying the water it'll make her sad. So he goes down to the well with me and I barely feel the weight of the empty bucket.

On the second trip I made, Mama looked at me all teary-eyed and she said to me, "All of the coleus plants have dried out completely." And she looked at Celestino again. So he went off and went inside the house.

"He's gone," I told my mother. And she said again, "All of them," and she started talking to herself and running her muddy hands all over her eyes and her face, like she was still a little child. I didn't feel like talking to her anymore, because lately she's gotten so weepy and blue that she cries over the least silly little thing. So then I went down to the well, on the third trip for water . . . I bumped into her there—floating on top of the water. And when without realizing what I was doing I hit her with the bottom of the bucket, she spoke to me, and her voice was like thunder, like she was speaking from the last room way way off down in a cavern—"All of them." And she started saying that, over and over and over again.

I tried to pull my mother out of the well. But she didn't want to come out. And she told me, with her face all wet (I don't know whether it was from tears or from the water), "Go away. I feel perfectly comfortable here."

So I went back with the buckets empty.

And as soon as I turned my back on the well I heard a great

Good God, betimes remove

The means that make us
                strangers!

— MACBETH, IV, iii

big huge sob coming out of it, and that made me so sad I tripped and fell, buckets and all. It made me so sad but I didn't want to go back to the well because she had told me in no uncertain terms to leave her be. So I went on up to the yard at the house with the buckets empty.

"But, young man, here you come with the buckets empty! What's wrong with you?" she said to me, surprised as could be, as she was replanting the coleus plants.

"Nothing! Nothing!" I said, and screaming real real softly, so that nobody (nor me either) could hear, I ran down to the well again, as fast as I could, and I filled up the buckets as fast as I could, all the time saying to myself, "What about Celestino? Where in the world has Celestino got off to?" . . . And I couldn't contain myself—I peeked down into the well. And there we were, the two of us huddled up together, shivering with the water up to our necks, and smiling at the same time, to show each other we weren't the least little bit scared.

You've started writing poetry again. And this time it's like you're more headlong and unstoppable than you ever were before. Now everybody in the country knows who you are. There's no way out anymore. Grandma says she feels like she could die of shame to think that a grandson of hers could take to such a thing. And Grandpa (with the hatchet always slung over his shoulder), he doesn't say anything but curse words.

You're writing poetry again, and I know you're never ever going to stop. It's just a lie that you plan to stop someday, even if you tell me you do; I know it's a lie. My mother knows it too, and all she does is cry. And my aunts, all they do is mutter.

And everybody hates you.

I can hear them now, muttering in the kitchen. Talking. Talking. Talking. They're trying to figure out a way to kill you. They're trying to figure out a way to kill you. They're trying . . .

If I could talk to you, I'd tell you something, except I don't know what it would be, but I can't anyway—they've sewed my mouth shut with a piece of barbed wire, and a witch with a stick is always right beside me, and the first "hmmmm" I try to make (which is the only thing I can say), the witch takes the stick and swishes it around over her head and gives me a whack with it. "Miserable whelp! All you ever do is spite me!"

What will we do now that everybody knows who we are! I'd bet practically anything that they're looking for us under the beds right now, and when they don't find us there, they'll look for us behind the chifforobe, and if we're not there—they'll climb up on the roof and look. And search. And hunt. And turn everything upside down looking. And they'll find us. There's no way out . . . And you still just keep on writing!

Today Celestino and I have spent the whole day taking red dirt out from behind the house to make a grand castle, exactly like the one he saw one time in a book with a lot of letters and colored pictures. Even prettier than that one! Because ours will be a *real* castle, not like that one he showed me that when all was said and done was pretty and all but it was still just colored paper.

"How many bedrooms are we going to make this castle have?"

"A hundred."

We're going to make this castle have a hundred bedrooms.

"And how many stories will the castle be?"

"Ten."

The castle is going to be ten stories tall.

"And how many towers?"

"Just one, but a great great big one."

We're just going to make this castle have one tower, but a great great big one—so big it's almost going to come up to the very top of the ceiba tree, because we're building the castle under the ceiba tree so we won't burn up in the sun. We've already piled up a whole lot of red dirt. Now we add water and stir it up, and we've got the cement. We picked up the rocks this morning. So we've got the materials together at the trunk of the tree. Now all we have left to do is start building. And bingo.

We've spent the whole day working on the big ten-story hundred-bedroom castle. All the jars and bottles are going to live in it. All the jars and bottles Grandma is saving in the sideboard, and that we intend to steal from her and bring here, because they'll be a whole lot more comfortable here than there in the sideboard where they're all squeezed in together and have to share the space with cockroaches and spiders that bite. But here, they'll live like kings . . . Except not all of them will be able to live so high. Celestino and I already have the way we're going to run the castle all planned out. First we're going to put in a king and a queen, and they'll live on the third floor. That whole floor will be just for them, and we're even going to put in a swimming pool and decorate the walls with all kinds of flowers, so it'll really look like the kind of place a king lives in. Then we're going to set up all the different kinds of princes—bad ones, good ones, ugly ones, young ones, and old ones. And then the princesses and the other kinds of people. We'll have to have them married so they'll all fit into the hundred bedrooms, because there are *so* many jars and bottles. Grandma has always collected them, even in the wild pineapple thickets, and the sideboard is packed full of bottles and jars, some of them all smelly and dirty and full of dead bugs.

It's almost dark, and we've got mud all over our faces, in our eyes, all over our bodies, but we're jumping for joy—we finally finished the red-dirt castle!

There it is, with its big tall tower. Even if it doesn't reach all the way to the top of the ceiba tree, it's a tall tall tower. There it is, with its hundred bedrooms and ten stories. All red, and decorated inside with lots and lots of crepe myrtle flowers, one on top of another so close that nobody would ever guess the walls are made out of red dirt and water. The Queen is so smug, walking all over the castle, inspecting and giving orders and sitting down and standing up again. She dives into the swimming pool and jumps out and dries herself off again. She gets dressed and takes off her clothes again. And then she goes out into the grand hall in front, from where you can see all the soldiers, marching and marching past, all in step, and never getting tired. We still haven't found the King we want, because we want the Florida Water bottle that Grandma's got hidden under her bed. She says there's a little perfume left. But we don't care—Celestino and I have it all planned, how we're going to put the Florida Water in another bottle and bring the bottle we want to the castle, and make it King. But so long as we don't have it, the Queen is the one in charge of giving orders.

Tonight there's a big party in the Red Dirt Castle. Even from far away you can see the torches winking and flashing in the four corners of the kingdom. The women all wear long dresses and lots of flowers on their bosoms and in their hair. The men all stand straight and tall and walk with their hands behind their backs, nodding and smiling little smiles that are more like they just stretch their lips a little—they never show their teeth. The music has started playing now for the first time, and from every floor more and more people come down the stairs, until the hall is full.

Celestino and I come to the door of the castle, to see the party and maybe have a piece or two of something sweet. We come to the door and try to go in, but the sentinels stop us with their big swords. They yell at us—"Back!"

"What geese!" I tell them. "Don't you see we're the ones that made this castle and even made *you!*"

But they answered us just the same way as they did before, yelling "Back!" at us, and they sounded so serious about it and pointed their spears so straight at our hearts that we didn't say another word. Celestino and I just looked at each other and turned around and started back down the grand staircase. It still had the

Sometimes
      a few birds,
      a horse,
have saved the ruins
of an amphitheatre.

—Jorge Luis Borges

smell of all the crepe myrtle flowers. And to think of all the work it took me to cut off the highest branches of the crepe myrtle bushes that had just flowered!

"Back!" yelled the sentinels at us again, even if we were already leaving. And all of a sudden I felt like laughing out loud. But I didn't, because I figured that would have made the guards even madder at me and they might even have killed me right there and then. When we got down to the lowest level, where the rocks that the big house was made out of first started rising up, we stopped. The far-off sound of the music came to us then, soft and far away and fading into the laughing and happy talk of the guests. We saw everybody come out onto the balconies all of a sudden and start dancing, almost in the dark. From time to time the music was clearer—except maybe that was just my imagination. Then again, you could just barely barely hear it. I looked at Celestino's face. He looked very very serious.

"What is it?" I asked him, without opening my lips.

"This castle is still not finished," he said, the same way I had talked to him.

"Why do you say that? What's missing?"

"Something very very important. What a couple of geese we've been!"

"What's missing? Tell me!"

"What do you think—the cemetery."

"Oh! That's right!"

And we stood there looking straight at each other, until we finally decided to open our lips and start talking.

"Tomorrow we have to finish the castle," Celestino told me out loud, since you could barely hear anything for all the music.

"What's missing?" I asked him, playing like I didn't know.

"The cemetery . . . ," he said offhandedly, as he chewed on the stalk of a mallow plant that had tiny little berries like buttons on it.

"Oh, that's right . . . ," I said. "Well, we can always do that tomorrow."

And we ran away from the ceiba tree, since now it was late at night and around that place, so people say, a woman all dressed in white with her hands stretched out like this in front of her comes out when it gets dark. And I don't know whether it's true or not, but my mother says whoever that woman smiles at wakes up dead.

Such fog this morning! We have to grope our way to the castle, and the only way we can tell which way to go is from the big white mass that sort of stands out from the fog, but just barely, and that if we're not mistaken is the ceiba tree. I can't see Celestino but I know he's right beside me because every once in a while I can hear him breathing. All the way from the house you can hear Mama's and Grandma's voices calling us like they were mad at us to come eat breakfast. But we don't pay them any mind. We're not hungry; what we want is to get to the ceiba tree as fast as we can and finish the castle so we can show it to our cousins, who'll be here any minute for the Christmas party.

Everybody's so excited about that party! Celestino and I made lists, and we asked them to get a lot of Christmas candy and even a bottle of wine, except it's pretty sure there's no way Grandpa will buy us a bottle of wine. But that doesn't matter—if he doesn't want to buy one for us we'll steal one Christmas Eve in the middle of all the fuss, when nobody's paying attention. This is the first Christmas Eve Celestino and I have spent together. We're going to have so much fun! . . . Mama's and Grandma's yelling and carrying-on gets louder now. The fog is lifting little by little. How nice!—the big white shape *was* the ceiba tree, and we almost trampled the castle down with our feet, we were so close to it.

"Young man, you better come eat right now if you plan to eat at all!"

"Ever since Celestino's been here he won't mind me for a minute!"

"Just our luck—inheriting that pest!"

"Young man! Young man . . . !"

Mama and Grandma have climbed up into the very highest part of the ceiba tree, and they're yelling and calling us from up there. But we just ignore them and play like we're deaf, because we don't want to waste any time—we still haven't made the

For a long time

you will learn

nothing but

how to

LAUGH

and

LAUGH.

— DASSINE

cemetery for the castle and we have to have it done by this afternoon.

Sweat is pouring off Celestino. He's gotten a big pile of rocks together and dug a great big huge hole, to take more red dirt out of so we can finish the cemetery, since what we had wasn't even enough for a good start, and he says the cemetery has to be big— a lot bigger than the castle, because they're going to be *here* a lot longer than they're going to be *there*, and they might as well be comfortable. Now Grandma and Mama have started throwing pieces of branches at us, and I'm thinking that the best thing for us to do is throw rocks at the two of them and see if we can't make them behave. But Celestino thinks we ought not to bother them, just ignore them up there, or at least so long as they don't mess up the walls of the castle.

We've finally finished the cemetery. It's so big! So big that even if you wanted to look at it all at once you couldn't, and I have to walk for a long time to get some idea of the size of it. I don't know, but if you ask me it's ridiculous. Where in the world are we going to get enough jars and bottles to bury in this cemetery? The ceiba tree is standing now in the middle of all the graves and Mama and Grandma, way high up in the branches, have started to cry. I feel so sorry for my mother, because I know how much the ceiba tree thorns must be sticking in her behind, but I can't go up there and help her because then if she gets down I'll have to stay up there by myself and I don't want to spend the rest of my life sitting in a ceiba tree, much less *this* ceiba tree, because Grandma says it's bewitched and it's the lightning rod for this whole part of the country. No. Let somebody else get struck by lightning. Not me.

"Come here, quick," Celestino says to me, from one of the corners of the cemetery. Covered with mud up to my neck, I run over to where he's waiting for me, sitting on top of the biggest tomb in the cemetery. "Look at what a big tomb," he says. "We didn't realize we were making it so big. I bet both of us together fit in here. Come on. Let's lie down and see for sure."

We've lain down in the big tomb all decorated with crepe myrtle flowers, and after two or three centuries I look at

Celestino and I scream and so then he looks at me and he screams too, as loud as he can. The chorus of witches comes up to us then, singing, singing, singing . . . The chorus of witches singing, and then giving us a big kiss . . .

The chorus of witches brought us a branch from a crepe myrtle bush today.

The chorus of witches danced through the big mud puddle.

The chorus of witches lay down with us and said, "Hello. Hello. Hello."

"It certainly is big," I said, laughing. And then he laughed out loud—so loud that my mother and grandmother got scared and took off flying, slipping away like two puffs of air, up away out of the ceiba tree.

"We both fit in here," we both said at the same time. And then we didn't say another word, because both of us already knew what the other one was going to say, so then what was the point of saying it? And we started trying to get an ant out that had sneaked into the tomb and filled it up almost completely. You ought to have seen him!—he was such a funny ant, and he said to us, "How are you doing?", and asked if he could step inside a minute and everything. But the darnedest thing of all was that when he asked if he could come in he didn't wait for an answer, he just came in. So now we're running around like a couple of madmen, trying to catch him, because he's quick as can be and he doesn't want to leave. Finally, between Celestino and me both, we grab him by the legs and hold him up in the air to swing him back and forth and throw him outside. And we were just about to fling him out when the ant started tickling us with his back legs, and we started laughing so hard that he slipped out of our hands. And now he's chasing us and tickling us, and neither Celestino nor I can stand the pain in our stomach, and we're still laughing, as hard as we can, such bellylaughs that we have to cover each other's ears with our hands. "What a stinking rotten ant," I say to myself, laughing all the while. And the ant, who must be a mind reader to boot, tickles me some more, and since I can't take any more, I start bawling and rubbing up against the wall, completely covered with crepe myrtle flowers. Until finally I guess the ant gets tired of tickling us and leaves us alone. But our giggle box is turned over, and we can't stop laughing, even if nobody is tickling us anymore.

"This heat is stifling. Let's throw off the covers."

"But we don't have on any covers . . ."

"I don't care, we're suffocating."

"It's that it's spring."

"That's just this part of the country for you."

"We've got to do something to change it."

"Uh-huh. Let's both think at the same time. We'll see what we can think of."

"Okay—go . . ."

"Are you thinking?"

"No."

"Me neither."

"Let's start again."

"Ready?"

"Not yet."

"I'm going to clap three times, and on the third clap we'll start."

"Ready?"

"Ready . . ."

Hatchets. Hatchets. Hatchets. Hatchets. Hatchets. Hatchets. Hatchets; hatchets; hatchets; hatchets; hatchets; hatchets; hatchets, hatchets, hatchets, hatchets, hatchets, hatchets, hatchetshatchetshatchetshatchetshatchetshatchets . . .

"It's almost daylight and I haven't slept a wink."

"Me neither."

"Did you think of something to make spring disappear?"

"Uh-huh."

"What?"

"Oh, now I've forgotten. But I know at midnight I got a wonderful idea! . . ."

"But why didn't you tell me *then*?"

"I *did*. Don't you remember?"

"No."

"Well I told you. It's that now you've forgotten too."

"Let's go to sleep again and see if the idea will come back to you. If it does, you call me as soon as it does."

"All right. I'm asleep."

"Me too."

"I'm dreaming."

"I'm dreaming."

"Here's the idea!"

"I hear it! But I forget it as soon as it comes. One word comes but then it goes pffft! and then here comes another one, and the only one I remember is the last one. Try to get a whole dream into one word and let's see if that way we can remember it."

"I can't."

"Try."

"I can't do it, it's a long long long dream."

"Dream . . ."

"I can't tell it in just one little word."

"Word . . ."

"I wish I could but I just cannot."

"Not . . ."

"I'll tell you how long the dream is—I just woke up and I still haven't finished the dream."

"Dream . . ."

Hatchets hatchets hatchets hatchets hatchets hatchets hatchets

"You—who are you?" I said.

"The elf," the elf said.

"What do you want?"

"The Queen's ring," he said.

"What Queen?"

"The one with the ring."

In January things change a whole lot. It may be hard to believe, but this is the only month that's not just like every other
month in the year. This one is different! Why? Oh, I wouldn't
know about why. But I know it's different. My aunt Adolfina
sings while she smears herself all over with white dirt. And
even my grandmother's voice when she calls me a corkhead and
whacks me with a fence post is different. Celestino changes too,
and even if he says that's foolishness, I know he changes. This
month he writes on the tree trunks just like always. But I don't
know . . . There's something different about the way he does it—
he doesn't write as fast as he does in the other months. Maybe
because this time of year there's less heat. Or maybe because the
thickets of wild pineapples are covered with little bellflowers and
they get so white that you'd never know they were wild pineapple
thickets; you'd think they were mountain after mountain after
mountain of all different sizes of little bellflowers. I like to try
to walk on top of the bellflowers without touching the ground,
and I always get Celestino to play too, and he's always the one
that loses because I know the game by heart so I know where to
put my feet. This month is really truly different! And now I don't
even remember that the Three Wise Men just went on by without
bringing me so much as a Communion wafer and that every day
we're starving to death more. This is such a nice month! It's a
shame there are years we don't have it . . . Now I can run and
run and run through the bileweed plants and roll around in them
and stand up and run again and climb up in the Indian laurel tree
and jump headfirst from way up there. Things are so pretty when
you look at them upside down, just a second before you crack
your skull on the rocks! I never get tired of climbing way way
up in the top of the Indian laurel and jumping headfirst so I can
see things in a different way. Until finally I've jumped so many
times they start looking the same as always, so then there's
nothing for me to do but keep walking with my feet down. But
that doesn't matter—sometimes Celestino and I get tired of walking with our feet down and of jumping from one pile of washed-
up rocks to another, holding on to the vines hanging off the trees
when we cross the bridge (made out of a piece of board) on one

foot while the stream murmurs down below there, saying to us, "Fall." "Fall. I'll smash you to pieces down here." We get tired of that. So then we start flying again, like in January. And we fly. Way way up, higher than the highest clouds. And we chase the buzzards and try to catch them, but all they do is look at us like they were scared . . . One day I caught a buzzard by the legs, when I was flying on top of the clouds. I did, I caught him and pulled on him as hard as I could. But all of a sudden the buzzard got so mad at me that he turned on me and started pecking at me. That was when I realized the buzzard I'd caught was my mother and my grandmother, flying around up there, because they'd had heaven only knows what kind of spell put on them.

So I flew a whole lot higher, trying to get away from that pecking.

"You miserable child," my mother and grandmother said over and over again, screeching in the clouds and fluttering and possessed by the devil. "Just let me catch you, and I'll smash you into the ground."

But they didn't catch me. I tumbled and somersaulted through the air and finally caught hold of the feet of a real live buzzard and got away clean by hanging on.

When I got to the ground I looked up and saw the great big buzzard of my mother and grandmother pecking at Celestino. So I tried to fly again so I could save him. But no matter how hard I tried and tried and tried I couldn't, and then just as I thought I was finally going to be able to, here came Grandpa and he sat on the stool he always sits on and he said to me, "Bring me some water to wash my feet with." So I went and brought him the water, and when I looked up at the sky again the buzzards had disappeared, and Celestino too . . . This month of January is so beautiful, really! Celestino gets up bright and early, picks up the butcher knife, walks down to the creek bed, and starts scribbling on the tree trunks. I get up bright and early too and go keep a lookout halfway down the road, and when I see Grandpa coming with the hatchet over his shoulder, I run and tell Celestino and the two of us run away and hide behind the clumps of pampas grass. This is really the very best month of all! Celestino whistles and everything, while he's scribbling, and I start feeling happy.

So happy, that I think one day he'll actually finish writing and when that happens we'll be able to sit in the round hollow part of the husk of a palm branch and slide down the hills again, and make a castle a whole lot bigger than the one we had planned. I think about all that, and so he'll finish faster I ask him if he wants me to help him. He always says he does, but as you know I don't know how to write so I can't say anything . . . So then that makes me sad and I go back to watching the road. That's what I do to make myself forget I'm such a jackass. So I'm forgetting when all of a sudden I see a shape coming up the road and I start shaking because I figure it's Grandpa with the hatchet over his shoulder. But it's not—it's a real old little old man coming towards me. The little old man is tottering along, really, and every once in a while he stumbles and falls down. Every time he falls he jumps right up, laughs, and when the rock he tripped on is not too big, he puts it in his mouth and goes glup and swallows it. But when the rock is too big he stands on it and says some kind of gobbledygook that I can't understand the first word of no matter how sharp I prick up my ears. Finally he gets to where I am, after I can't tell you how many tumbles, cackles, and fits of gobbledygook.

"Great toothed fornivores!" he says, and he trips and falls and cracks his head on the ground right in front of my feet. But quick as a wink he gets back up again, looks at me for a couple of seconds as his smile fades away, and all of a sudden takes off down the riverbed like he'd seen a ghost. I just stand there with my mouth open watching him disappear into the tumbled rocks and washes. But a minute later I shake myself and run after him. And I finally catch up to him. The old man looks at me and then he sits down real real slow on the rocky ground where once in a while the river splashes up, and he starts to cry.

We cry almost till night. We cry, because I can't watch anybody cry without my own tears starting up on the spot. "That's a good habit to break," my mother always tells me when she sees me crying because other people are crying. But I like it. And besides, even if I didn't like it, I'd have to do it anyway.

"I am the month of January," the little old man says to me, and all of a sudden I realize I'm talking to a dead person. "Don't start bawling, please," the dead person begs me. "If you start bawling I'll start bawling too, because the minute I see somebody crying I start getting all teary too."

At that very minute Celestino was coming back from the mountain with his arms stretched out in front of himself and the awl, just like always, sticking out of the middle of his chest. Like a pin in a pincushion.

"I am the month of January," the dead person said to me again.

Celestino came over to me, with his arms out: "I am the month of January."

Jumping from rock to rock, running through the rocky ravines and in and out the tree trunks, Celestino and I cross the pasture. The dead person is still chasing us, and once in a while he gives a wavery bawl.

"He's the month of January," I tell Celestino, but what I want to tell him is "Why don't we wait for him—he's been so nice to us," but Celestino doesn't hear me, he just keeps looking at the moons.

"Last night," he says, "I called you so many times to go look for one of the moons. But you just didn't want to wake up."

"You must have been dreaming, because I didn't sleep a wink last night."

"No, I know I wasn't dreaming, because the spiders were walking around just like always—all over the roof of the house . . ."

"I am the month of January . . ."

"Then how could I not have waked up if I wasn't asleep."

"You might have been dreaming that you weren't asleep."

"No, because I saw the spiders, too, as clear as day, sneaking across behind the night—up above the roof."

"I am the month of January!"

The dead person starts looking tinier and tinier and tinier, he's falling so far behind. Celestino has gotten awfully sad, because there was one second I looked back and waved at the dead

It all comes back
    to his memory now.
Unable to stop himself,
    he sighs and weeps.

— Song of Roland

man to come on. He's the month of January, I said to Celestino, to make him feel better. But he ignored me and just kept being sad. Almost at daybreak we came to the house, because we had gone a long way off without realizing it, and the trip back always seems to take longer than the going away. And we got the houses mixed up quite a few times and went up to some of them, thinking they were ours. At one of them we came to we went to bed, and it wasn't till after we were in bed that we realized it wasn't ours, because there wasn't a single spider on the roof. Celestino was already practically asleep when I told him it looked to me like we weren't in our own bedroom. He jumped straight up in bed, stuck his head out the chinks in the walls, and said, "You're right"; so we ran out of that strange, awfully strange, house that was so much like our own. Except I don't understand how we could get mixed up like that, because that house had the well in the parlor and sitting on the wellhead was a little itty-bitty woman pulling up water in a bottle. When she saw us come out of the bedroom the woman hid behind the well and then she started yelling and screaming. She said, "There they go! There they go! That way!" And she was right—there we went, running as hard as we could. But we finally got to our own house! There is such a big silence! The bedbugs aren't even hopping in the mattress when Celestino and I, completely worn out, fall into bed at the same instant and pull the sheet right up over our heads.

"How peculiar that Grandpa didn't put a hatchet under the pillow!"

"That's right! He must have forgotten."

"Do you think one day you'll be able to finish what you're writing? I'm getting more scared every day—Grandpa's on our trail, and any second he could catch us and chop us into sausage meat."

"I'm not sure how much I still have to go. But I feel like I've just barely started!"

"I don't think there's any way out for us anymore—just yesterday I saw Grandma bury a live pigeon in the kitchen . . ."

"Impossible!"

"Uh-huh. I saw her."

"Poor pigeon. Why didn't you dig her up?"

"I started to, but then I got too scared. And Grandma, who

you'd think was a mind reader, picked up the paring knife and said to me, 'I dare you to dig up that live pigeon. I'll catch you and slit your throat like a sheep.' And I didn't dare dig it up, because she would have done what she said. The expression on her face would've scared off anybody."

"Let's go get it out! Come on!"

"It must be dead by now."

"No, I'll bet it's still wheezing."

What a silly idea of Celestino's—a pigeon Grandma buried yesterday morning, to think it would still be alive today. But I go into the kitchen with him all the same, because I'm too scared to stay in the bedroom by myself, what with the way things are in this house. When it's not a woman all dressed in white it's a dog that talks like a person, or a spider with a person's head—something always appearing before us.

No, I wouldn't stay there by myself if you paid me.

"Are you sure it was the kitchen she buried the pigeon in?"

"Uh-huh, as sure as I'm standing here. She buried it right by the front legs of the cookstove."

"What cookstove?"

"The cookstove."

"There's no cookstove here!"

Celestino and I have put our arms real tight around each other, and we can feel each other shaking and hear our teeth rattling from how scared we are. We've gotten the houses mixed up again. Huddled together, groping in the empty air, we try to invent the cookstove, until we hear a loud long laugh practically right on top of us. The month of January appears before us, holding a kerosene lantern.

"Come," he says. "I watched you lie down a while ago in my bed, and I went out onto the porch to catch moths with the lantern, because the poor things always fly around and around the light of a lantern until they can't fly another inch and then they dive into the lantern, straight for the wick. Come, the lantern's almost out of kerosene."

Now we run around and around and around the lantern, and now we're going so fast we look like we're standing in the same place.

I look at the wick, and I know it's just a matter of seconds before I make one last effort and dive at it headfirst. I look at the wick. I go around two or three more times in one second and then, finally, I dive at the fire. Celestino gives a yell, and the flame goes out before I get to it.

"Well, have it your own way," the month of January tells us, and he tosses the lantern into a corner. "Have it your own way this time, but listen now and I'll tell you a word you'll forget as soon as you hear it. Listen to it . . . You've already forgotten. One day you'll remember which word it was that I said to you, and on that day both of you will burn yourselves up alive."

And he said the word.

And we forgot it as soon as he said it.

And we bolted out of the house like two madmen, while the month of January laughed big long loud bellylaughs and yelled, "One day you'll remember that word I told you. One day you'll remember."

So finally we came to our own house. Because it couldn't be any other house but our house, that one, that as soon as we went into we saw ourselves asleep in bed, with our heads all covered up and dreaming and dreaming and dreaming that we had forgotten all the words in the world and the only way we could understand each other now was by talking with our hands and making faces.

THE END

Now we are really starving. Not a stalk of the corn that came up was finally left standing, and in the sideboard there's not a morsel to sink your teeth into. Grandma has kept getting skinnier and skinnier and skinnier, and now she can hardly stand on her own two feet. Poor Grandma. Just yesterday she fell down in front of the cookstove and she couldn't get up again, she was so hungry. Then Mama went over to help her up, but she was so skinny and weak by now too that she went down next to Grandma. The two of them, there on the floor not able to get up again, simply looked at each other a second. And I saw a kind of lightning-bolt flash from Mama's eyes into Grandma's eyes. But I couldn't show anybody because the lightning bolt disappeared like a streak. So then I felt like I should pick Mama and Grandma up. I wanted to, too, but I didn't want to at the same time, because I figured if I tried to pick them up I'd fall like they had and I wouldn't be able to get up either.

And now that we are really and truly starving, all my aunts have hotfooted it out of the country and they don't stop by even to say hello anymore. They went off with the first one that looked at them a second time. Just Adolfina has stayed, bringing in white dirt to fill up the holes all over her face . . . Grandpa headed out for the mountain early this morning, to see if he could find something to eat, and now he's back again with the sack over his shoulder—empty. "What will become of us," I heard Grandpa say behind the stone-cold cookstove, and even though he never cries he almost broke down. And then he went out into the yard, but by now there's not a tree or anything else left in the yard because he's cut them all down. Grandpa kept walking, all over the yard, and then he went down to the well. He stayed there awhile, leaning on the wellhead palings. And finally he took the bucket, lowered it all the way to the bottom, pulled it up full of water, and drank and drank and drank till his stomach was full.

Celestino doesn't say a word, but I know he can't take much more. I go out onto the road to beg for pennies with a cup, but there's nobody that'll give me so much as a plug nickel. And it's because we're not the only ones starving, the whole country is, because not a drop of rain has fallen in this part of the country for more than two years, so there's not a cow left on four legs, and even the few trees far off there that Grandpa hasn't cut down and that have leaves too bitter to eat are turning yellow and withered. At home we all go to bed early to see if we can't dream about food—but even that doesn't work, because we're all so hungry we can't sleep a wink. I sit down to think—and I think, and I worry, and I think, and the only conclusion I can come to is that we have to eat Grandpa, who's the oldest, so he's lived the longest. That's what I think, but I don't say it to anybody. And too, that kind of thing scares me to death, because if we start with the oldest ones, pretty soon it'll be my turn. Sooner or later somebody would come along and say to me, "Time to eat you, since you're the oldest now." That's why I don't tell anybody about this crazy idea of mine—but as hard as I try to make it go away, it still keeps running around and around in my head. And sometimes I wish I could tell Celestino my idea, to see what he'd say about it.

First thing in the morning we all go off to the mountain, to see if we can find something to eat. Grandpa was the first one to find something—an almond seed under a rock, and for the life of me I can't figure out how in the world it got under there. But Grandpa didn't get to eat the seed, because Grandma, who was scrabbling around close to him, snatched it out of his hands. So then this great big wrangle started between the two of them, and Mama went over, using two thistle sticks for crutches, and grabbed away the almond seed and swallowed it in one gulp. So then Grandma started fighting with my mother, just barely whispering because she didn't have the energy to yell anymore but still furious, and then she bent over and started scrabbling around on the ground again because she said she'd seen an almond seed roll between her feet and dig a hole and crawl into it, scared to death. But nobody paid her any mind because that was probably just hunger talking, making her see visions . . . About noon Celestino and I discovered a green leaf on a breakax tree and we ran over to climb the tree to get it, but when we got to the top we saw it wasn't a leaf at all, it was a beautiful bird. As soon as it saw us it flew away and disappeared. Celestino and I looked at each other, very serious, and we didn't know what to say to each other. We both thought the same thing—*This hunger is making us see all kinds of strange, strange things.* What does that bird live on, I said when we'd climbed down out of the tree.

We haven't found anything all day long . . . And to think it's been more than a hundred years since we had a bite to eat! By now we've almost gotten used to living on air, as my mother said. When she still had the strength to talk.

Now everything has sunk into such a terrible calm that I ask myself whether we may not all have died and that's why a hundred years have gone by, just like that, one after another, and we're still on our feet more or less and looking for something to eat. We don't sleep anymore. A long time ago we gave up on feeling sleepy, so now we don't sleep anymore. Now the only thing we do is go outside and spend all day looking for food, even though we've never found anything.

Now we walk on all fours like dogs. Yes, if I don't misremember, dogs were these creatures that walked on four feet, like butterflies. I think that's right, but I'm not sure—we ate the last dog that dared to bark at us so long ago that I really don't recall what shape it was. But I think it was like this—it had a white, real white face and it was almost always smiling, it walked on four feet, not because it couldn't walk on two (because when it wanted to, it could fly and everything), but because it was a big coward and didn't feel safe when it walked on just two. The last dog there was in the world, according to what my grandfather told me, with signs, dragged itself along the ground, like a boa constrictor, from how scared it was of everything . . . But we don't crawl because we're scared; it's because we're hungry, and I know in my own mind that before, when our stomachs were full, we did whatever we wanted to. And one time I wanted to go to the moon, so I went to the moon. But as soon as I got there I turned around and came back, because I'd no more than set foot on it when I saw my grandmother, my mother, all my aunts, and my grandfather, all sitting on a big rock that was flickering like a lightning bug. Like a lightning bug . . . Like a lightning bug? . . . Yes, just like a night lightning bug; because there are day lightning bugs too—even if nobody has ever seen one, I know there are some, and I know the day lightning bugs are the cockroaches that since they can't light up, people kill them.

"We've been waiting for you for better than a thousand years," my mother said as soon as I set foot on the moon. I got so scared when I heard her say "a thousand years" that I went back home in one jump. And when I got home, my mother was standing behind the door holding out her arms to me and she said, "You've finally come—we've been waiting for you for better than a thousand years."

So then I screamed. Yes, I remember I screamed real loud. But Celestino was still alive then, and he smiled at me. He smiled at me and said, "Hi," when everybody else had talked to me about waiting a thousand years. That was when I realized that all of this was just some of Grandma's hexing, because when he said "Hi" he was smashed to smithereens. Hi.

All he said was Hi, like it wasn't five minutes ago I left home.

Now I'm getting ready for when I have to start crawling, because I don't think I can take much more walking on four feet. The whole family is in the same situation I am, so we're practicing, a little every day—putting our stomach on the ground and crawling along real slow, like some just-hatched lizards . . . and Grandpa even tried to cut off my head because he said he'd gotten me mixed up with a real lizard. I broke out laughing, but then I got serious, because I figured out that Grandpa hadn't really mixed me up with anybody, he'd just wanted to catch me off guard so he could cut off my head and once I was dead eat me . . . Uh-huh, that's even worse, how scared we are of each other. If it wasn't that I was so scared that the others would eat me and they weren't so scared that I'd eat them, we might even be able to sleep for a while. But fat chance of *that!* Who's about to go to sleep in this house if somebody's always watching you with their eyes on fire and their mouths watering? Mine too.

"Now a person's got to be more careful than ever," I tell Celestino, but not by words.

"You've got to be careful even of *me*," he always answers me, the same way I talk to him.

"And you of *me*," I say to him, by thought again.

That's how far things have gone in this house.

Grandma still hasn't lost that mania she has of making signs of the cross in the air, and one day she said she'd seen a saint that came up to her and touched her face and said, "You are still very beautiful." We all laughed at Grandma's latest crazy saying. And I figured the saint was real fat and we could have eaten him, and I made signs till Grandma understood me.

So then she said, "Animals!" and we all jumped, we were so surprised she could talk so loud.

"Animals!" she repeated, but this time real soft. And then she went dumb again.

But dumb and all, she still opened and closed her mouth and called us "animals," even though you couldn't really hear her. So now every time she sees us she starts opening and closing her mouth, like a little lizard chick when it's real hot outside. I feel so sorry for Grandma, such an old little old thing, and still alive! Is it possible that we're never ever going to die? That's what I'm afraid of—that we might be eternal, because then there's really truly no way out. But I ought not to worry about that—we're not going to be eternal, because Grandpa hasn't gotten up off the floor for a long long time now, and although sometimes he crawls along a little ways, he never manages to walk a foot. We all watch Grandpa with fire in our eyes and our mouths watering. But so far we still can't . . .

. . .

Celestino gave me one of his ears tonight. "Here, this is for you." I told him I'd save it for later, but I took it and swallowed it in one gulp as soon as he gave it to me.

Grandpa looks like he's just barely wheezing. My mother has brought in the big hatchet he cut down so many trees with, and she shoos us away with it and tells us, "Just hold your horses there, I'm going to do the dividing up." That's what she tells us, without opening her mouth, because we've learned how to talk that way now, and we all understand each other fine. But I can't help worrying, because I know she's gotten tricky lately, and the day we all agreed to cut off our big toes and make a stew out of them, she cut off her little toe instead and then said she'd gotten mixed up. So that's why I don't trust her too much anymore, and I know she's been watching me with her eyes sparkling and her mouth watering, like she was eating me inside her head. But she better not think she's going to get her own way this time, because I'm not budging an inch from here till Grandpa has breathed his last—and then I'll be the first one to jump up and get the part that rightfully should come to me and eat and eat and eat till I'm stuffed and then can say *Celestino* like before . . . How do you think you say the word *Celestino*? . . . When I imagine myself saying it I feel so happy I can't contain myself and I start dancing, crawling through the dust and licking the floor with my tongue to sharpen it up so when the day comes when I can talk again I can talk real sharp and clear.

Grandpa's coming to the end now and we're all hanging over him drooling, waiting for the moment. Adolfina, whiter than ever, has dragged in her sewing scissors. My mother raises the hatchet now, and Grandma, opening and closing her mouth, crawls closer and closer and finally starts gnawing on his foot. Celestino closes his eyes and cries inside. I look at Grandpa's face and eyes, that are finally flickering faster and faster until they give off a whole lot of sparks and just freeze open.

The moment has come.

And we all attack him like a bunch of wild animals. Food!

DO NOT BOAST OF THY
MIGHT, FOR THOU CANST
NOT KEEP DEATH FROM
EXTINGUISHING THY DAYS
AND THY NIGHTS, WHICH
SLINK AWAY, ONES LIKE
WHITE SLAVES AND THE
OTHERS LIKE BLACK.

— Moussa - Ag - Amastan

Food after so long—except I don't know how to gauge the time and so I can't really say so. My mother gave a whack with the hatchet and we all fell to, like an army of fire ants, till there wasn't even a bone left. Adolfina gave a couple of clicks with her sewing scissors at Grandpa, like he was a piece of worn-out sheet, grabbed her part, and went off looking down her nose at the rest of us. The minute Grandma tasted the first bite she got all her strength back and more, and the first thing she did when she could talk again was say "Shit." Then she said "Animals," "Animals," "Animals," till she was a little calmer and went and settled down in a corner, where she cried all that afternoon and night. By the time Mama's belly was full she was crawling as good as new—because it appears she forgot how to walk the other way—and she crawled down to the well, where she said she was going to have a drink of water, except later I found out the well was dry. Celestino and I looked at each other and in one hop we were out, both at once, out through the roof of the house, and as quick as a wink we had gotten high high up, higher than the highest clouds . . . And now we're way up here, trying to find out why it is that it never rains anymore. And we keep going higher, until we lose sight of the mountain, the brown and yellow ground, and everything that's not us ourselves and the ground we're standing on. But then we keep on going higher.

"Madre mía!" Celestino said. "Look at that big river coming at us!"

I was going to say something, since it didn't look to me like any river, but the chorus of cousins came over to me and said, "Let's go," and since I held back a little they dragged me bed and all and threw me down plump on the roof of the house, where they had landed before I had.

"Do you still want to kill Grandpa?" they asked me.

"Uh-huh," I said.

"Then pay attention and try to sleep more than you dream."

And they disappeared into the termite-eaten thatch of the roof, like a bunch of cockroaches, those that hide at the first whiff of rain. And it rained. And rained. And rained. So, so much that the water came up very slow and pompous to the roof and kissed me and circled my throat several times.

. . .

After we said goodbye to January, Celestino and I started writing that interminable poetry again, and more furiously than ever. The elf has come back once or twice, but he hasn't asked me for the ring. And my mother and grandfather have declared open war on us and are just looking for an excuse to club us and pull off our ears. Adolfina doesn't just paint her face and arms with white dirt now, she paints the whole house and the parlor and breezeway floor. Poor Grandma slipped and fell headlong into the well. One day it had been raining a lot and Grandpa made her go get a bucket of water, because he said he wasn't about to wash his feet in the rainwater that ran out of the gutters on the roof into the rain barrel because the gutters were always full of cat shit. And even though the house was flooded with rainwater, he just kept saying like the stubborn old goat he is that it had to be wellwater. But since Grandma was still grumbling, he took the machete scabbard and whacked her two or three times across the back and said, "Get," and then he whacked her four times and said "Get" again. "Get, unless you want your neck wrung." So Grandma went out with the bucket on the pole, the pole over her shoulder, and her hands at her throat. And the only thing we heard was the "sshp" she made when she fell into the well. But we didn't hear another thing. Not a shout or anything. And I can't stop worrying about why Grandma didn't yell before she hit bottom, because now I'm thinking that she might have dropped a rock in the well and she's really in hiding, somewhere out there in a cave or something, and just biding her time till we're all asleep so she can come in and cut off our heads. That's what I've been thinking, and I already told Celestino, but he told me not to worry about such foolishness, that Grandma was at the bottom of the well sure as sure can be. But I still have my doubts, and one of these days I'm going to dry out the well to see if she's really at the bottom. For the time being I always wrap my head up in the sheets, except it's as hot as Hades and I get sopping wet from sweat. But a lot of times I don't have time to think whether Grandma is alive or dead because Mama and Grandpa (who you better believe are very much alive) are more dangerous than she is, and they spend the whole day trying to kill us, in

112

twenty different ways. Now neither Celestino nor I shut our eyes all night, and we're always thinking that any second Grandpa will come to the door with the hatchet raised over his head and chop us into kindling.

These last few days the fog has come back. And Grandma has come back too. She showed up one afternoon, while we were eating. When Grandpa saw her he gave a yell like a cat somebody had poured scalding water on. But Grandma said to him, "Don't be scared, you old bastard, I'm just a ghost." And she sat down at the table. And I guess it's true that she was a spirit, because she didn't have a bite to eat. And her the biggest glutton that ever walked the face of the earth when she was alive! So she must have been dead as a doornail not to stuff herself with a mess of corn and boiled plantain. My mother didn't pay her the least bit of mind, she just looked right through her like she wasn't there. "This miserable daughter of mine doesn't even forgive me dead," Grandma said and she went out in a cloud of smoke by the kitchen door. We just kept on eating. And Grandpa, who by now had calmed down some, said it was a disgrace and that *that woman* didn't give him a minute's peace even when she was dead. Later it got to be night and my mother made me go down to the well to bring up some water to water the flowers with.

By now everybody knows that Celestino is a poet. The news has spread through this whole part of the country so now everybody knows it. My mother says she'll die of shame, she'll never be able to set foot out of the house again. Adolfina says that's the reason she can never get a husband, and even my dead grandmother has shut herself up in the corn press and says she won't come out even if she comes back to life. The milkmen don't buy the milk that our cows give from Grandpa anymore, and when the milkmen go by the house they throw rocks at us and yell, "There goes the poet's family." And they roar with laughter as they go on past.

In the whole house all you hear is the pss-pss-pss of my family with their heads together trying to figure out a way to make Celestino disappear.

"We've got to kill him," Grandpa says.

"Animals!" dead Grandmother answers him, but she disagrees just for the sake of disagreeing, because then she chuckles and she says, "Just leave it to me, I'm the one with the most experience . . ."

"Throw him in the well," my mother says. And all of a sudden all you can hear is her voice growing and growing till we're all deaf, "Throw him in the well, throw him in the well."
"Throw him in the well."

Celestino has heard that voice too. It doesn't seem to come out of anybody's throat at all, you'd think it came out of some horrible animal, and as hard as I try to imagine what it looks like, I can't quite see it. So I try again. But no luck . . .
"Throw him in the well."
"Throw him in the well."

Rockaby baby in the treetop,
When the wind blows the cradle will rock,
When the bough breaks the cradle will fall,
And down will come baby, cradle and all.

I've forgotten that song now. I'll go over to where my mother is, over there weaving a new straw seat for the rocking chair, and I'll ask her to tell me how it goes.

"Mama, I've forgotten that song Rockaby Baby. Why don't you tell me how it goes again."

"What a child! You and your whining! It's all my own fault for spoiling you so. Come on, climb up here on my lap."

Mama has sat me on her lap. And she's started singing. My mother is so good. I still like for her to sing to me and carry me. Except I know Mama always has work to do. But at night I whimper some and she comes to where I am and asks me what the matter is and she picks me up and carries me over to the rocking chair that rocks and she tells me a story . . . While Mama rocks me on the chair and sings Rockaby Baby or something, Celestino gets more and more serious and just sits there on the doorsill beam in the parlor. Poor Celestino! He doesn't have anybody to sing him even Three Blind Mice, and he always has to sleep by himself and nobody ever runs their hand over his head.

"Why don't you rock Celestino too, Mama?"

"It's that he's a big boy now."

"No, he's still as little as I am. Look at him."

"He's big. Go to sleep, now, it's late."

We're all going crazy, so people say. The only person who doesn't think so is my mother, who still carries me once in a while and tells me a story and everything. Except she usually falls asleep before I do.

Grandpa has found some tree trunks written on and it's made him as mad as a bull. "Folderol," he says, "some pea-brain is writing folderol." I don't know, but there must be something from way back that makes Grandpa so mad when he sees the trees all carved up. If that wasn't what it was, why would he get that way? Uh-huh, there must be something I don't know about.

"Pick me up," I said to my mother. And she said, "The devil with you, leave me alone." I looked at her real good, because I didn't think that was my mother. And sure enough it wasn't, even if she did have the same voice and face and body. But her feet had turned into two big stingers like a scorpion, and two blind snakes flicking their tongues were coming out of her eyes. "Mama," I said, and the two snakes hid their tongues, but they kept looking at me.

· · ·

Celestino is crying, out behind the privy. I go and ask him why he's crying, but he won't answer me, so then I don't know what to do, and so I start crying too, till Grandpa finds us and says, "Sissies, here you are crying again. If I catch you, I'm going to string you up." Celestino and I take off running and climb up to the very top of the ceiba tree. And we stay up there in the leaves, real quiet and peaceful, and sure Grandpa is not about to find us up here. And we keep on crying a little, soft so nobody will find out.

From the mountain the cows come down dressed in white. In white the cows down from the mountain. Come.

We've taken our nap under the yagrumo tree. We wake up and then go back to sleep. We do that every morning, afternoon, and night. And now that the sun is coming up, we lie back down again. And we doze a while longer.

While we were asleep a witch came along and poked us with her broomstick. The witch said, "It's too late," and flew off on her broomstick. I called Celestino and asked him if he had seen her too, but when I opened my eyes I realized I was still asleep and I couldn't ask him anything.

Dressed in white, all the cows in long lines, in long lines, in long line . . .

Then I looked up and I saw Celestino way up high, galloping along behind the witch. Straddling a broom too.

From the mountain, from the mountain . . .

· · ·

"Don't you ever intend to give me the ring?" said the elf.

"You must have the wrong person, sir. I don't have any ring to give you."

"Idiot! I'm never wrong! You're the one that's given the wrong answer!"

I found all this out from a woodpecker that lives in one of the holes in the yagrumo tree, and he told me everything. If he hadn't, I'd never have heard a thing about it. The woodpecker also told me that he planned to make so many holes in the yagrumo tree that there would come a moment when the tree would just disappear, and then he'd have a hole so big that nobody could even see it, and everybody would think he was living in the air.

I didn't know what to do, the woodpecker stopped talking. So then I asked Celestino what I could do. And he told me, "Kill him, what he said was bad."

So we killed the bird. Except the hole was already made before the bird told us about it. It wasn't him that made it, not even close.

"Tomorrow we're going to buy you a pair of shoes," my mother said before she covered me up with the sheets. Then she stayed with me awhile till finally I was falling asleep and I saw her getting blurrier and blurrier right in front of my eyes. Then my grandmother appeared and said, "Spoiled wart, you think you're the king of this whole house. Well, enough! Starting tomorrow you get up first thing in the morning and go out with your grandfather to bring in the calves and help him milk the cows, since that la-de-da cousin of yours isn't worth his keep, and if it's not one thing it's another—if he's not vomiting up a tapeworm it's diarrhea or fever—but the fact is that he can never do what you tell him to do. Miserable family—nobody worth a plug nickel! And I know it's all my own fault for marrying that sickly grandfather of yours. So don't say I didn't tell you—tomorrow first thing in the morning I'm going to get you up. I've had enough of your laziness! If you don't work you're not getting any food from *me*—you or your mother either."

First thing in the morning my mother came to where I was half asleep and she said to me real low, "Get out of bed. Your grandfather is already asking where you are." So I got out of bed and I put my arms around her. I could feel her sort of trembling inside. But I didn't say a word to her because I think I must have been trembling too, and if I had told her so she probably would have started crying. Because lately my mother has taken to sniffling. Right this minute, as I'm trying to find a stubborn jackass of a calf in these rocks and boulders, I know that my mother is out crying behind the corn press or leaning against the wellhead. My mother cries, and I don't know what to say to her or what to do. And the worst part of it is that if my grandfather sees her crying he throws such a fit you'd think he was going to kill himself or her, and he starts hitting her in the face. Jackass of a calf, wait till I catch you. I'm going to stone you to death.

"Look, Mama, I picked these sweetsops up on the mountain and brought them to you."
"How nice. They're so good."

"There's that ninny son of yours again with that stinking fruit. All you do is fill this house up with garbage. Tell him to throw them out this minute."
"Throw them away!"
"No, I brought them to you to eat."
"Throw those sweetsops out right this minute! Here comes your grandfather."

Tonight I can't sleep, even if I close my eyes and sometimes even rub them with my fingers. Mama has come over to me several times and said to me, "Throw those sweetsops away." "Throw those sweetsops away." Then my grandfather comes in with a piece of rope and says, "The time has come to hang your mother. Come with me so you can make the noose for her."

.   .   .

"Make the noose for me," said my mother, who appeared all of a sudden at the ceiling. Already hanging from the roof beam.

Then Grandfather came in holding a chamberpot. "Drink, you motherless child."

So I drank.

Then I put my arms around Celestino, and I could finally go to sleep, so the witch tells it, and she goes everywhere with me now.

"You're the only thing I have, my son."

"Yes, Mama."

"You should always love me."

"Yes, Mama."

"If you left me I don't know what would become of me."

"Yes, Mama."

"You're the only thing I have . . ."

"Oh, this itch where I can't get at it to scratch!"

Now there are just a few days left before Christmas. Just a few days. Then all my cousins and aunts will come. What a big party. I don't intend to go out looking for stray calves that day even if Grandpa takes the strap to my back till I'm black and blue . . . The witch that's always with me has punched me awake and she's laughing and clambering up on the bed railing. Celestino is still asleep. Poor thing. Last night he must have been very very sick because all he did was moan and go out to the privy six or seven times. It makes me so sad to see how skinny Celestino has gotten. You can count his ribs. And that's even when at night sometimes I get up and steal some food out of the kitchen and bring it to him to eat. But it doesn't seem to work—every day he gets skinnier. It makes me so sad to see him. He's down to skin and bones. And it's all Grandpa's fault—he doesn't let him eat a bite, with the looks he gives him every time he sits down at the table. Uh-huh, because even if Grandpa won't tell him straight out to get lost, not to eat, as soon as Celestino comes to the table he starts acting like a mad dog. He throws the spoons and slams down the soup so it splashes all over the table and starts looking daggers at Celestino, like he'd done something terrible and Grandpa was blaming him. And poor Celestino, who doesn't know a thing in the world, he thinks it's true that it's his fault, so he goes off to the kitchen crying. And then Grandpa says he can't take *that boy* anymore, that he won't eat just to mortify and spite him, and saying he's going to make Celestino eat, he goes off to the kitchen too and starts hitting and kicking him. While Grandpa is kicking Celestino in the kitchen, Adolfina sings with her mouth closed, she says so she won't get wrinkles; my mother cries very soft, still eating, and Grandma scolds her and says, "Fool, you silly fool." Then I get very very still, and I hear poor Celestino puffing and breathing hard as he rolls on the floor and Grandpa kicks him and kicks him . . . Every time this happens (and it happens every day) my dead cousins start coming down off the roof, and they sit down at the table and eat and eat and eat, because they say now they have to eat everything my grandfather didn't let them eat before, when they were alive and got kicked.

The thuds of Grandpa's kicks are drowned out by Celestino's grunts and puffs.

Now my dead cousins come down.

Grandma slaps Mama and says Fool to her more than a hundred times, till she gets herself so worked up she breaks a plate over her head and throws hot flour in her eyes.

The witch got scared off. And when I saw her leave I got so so scared too, because I figured she probably was never going to come back again.

I think what Celestino has is that his insides have burst from Grandpa kicking him. Yes, that must be what he's sick from.

Dinner again. And again the kicking. One of my dead cousins has looked at me sniffling with my eyes full of tears and told me, "Crybaby." Then at a signal all of them disappear. But the word *crybaby* has stayed, and it grates on my ears.
Crybaby. Crybaby. Crybaby.

. . .

THOU CANST NOT DENY

THAT THY FAITHFULLEST SERVANT

IS THY SHADOW, THAT KEEPS

A CARPET ALWAYS UNDER

THY FEET.

— Moussa-Ag-Amastan

Now I know what my cousin meant by that word *crybaby*. Tomorrow, at dinnertime, I'll come to an understanding with them . . . Celestino moans more than ever tonight. Tomorrow I'll have a talk with my dead cousins.

Thank goodness! I'm so happy; the witch woke me up this morning with the same beating as always!

I've discovered that my mother has stopped talking to me. According to what the witch tells me, it's that she's jealous of Celestino.
"That's a lie!" I say to the witch.
"You know it's true."
"I love her."
"And she loves you, too."
"Then why doesn't she talk to me?"
"Because she knows you love Celestino better."

Now, after so long, I realize that my mother is crazy as a loon. Poor thing, it must be from the hunger she's been through, or maybe for want of a husband. Going by what the witch told me, that's terrible for a woman. I'm so lucky not to be a woman.

Now we're in the dining room. Celestino, like always, is the last one to come to the table. As soon as Grandpa sees him, he starts grumbling and muttering. Celestino sits down, and Grandpa curses and throws a crow into the middle of the table. Celestino doesn't dare reach to get himself anything to eat. Grandpa drops his plate. It lands on the floor and he starts arguing with Celestino, because he says it's *his* fault. "Goddamn child, always mixing me up!" Celestino goes over trembling and picks the pieces of china up off the floor. Grandpa starts slapping him in the face. My mother's eyes are brimming over with tears by now. Adolfina starts singing. The witch, like always, slips away through the roof. And now here come my dead cousins! . . .

They're more raucous than ever and they start scrounging around all over the table, spilling and turning things over, and they eat literally everything, even Grandpa's crow.

Grandpa drags Celestino into the kitchen, hitting him with his fists all the way, and once there he starts kicking him.

The cousin that called me a crybaby yesterday comes up to me and says it to me again.

"No," I say then.

"Why not?" all my dead cousins say to me.

"Because I want to kill that grandfather."

All my cousins stop eating, jump up, and pick up the big clay bowl and put it on my head.

"We crown you," they say, and run off and hide up on the roof. "See you tonight."

The clay bowl falls off my head and smashes to smithereens on the floor. Grandma starts scolding.

"What in the world gave you the notion to put a bowl on your head! You pig! That's no hat. Now we'll have to serve our food up in a chamberpot. You good-for-nothing ninny! What you need is to be beat till you bust!"

And she starts slapping me, cursing me with every slap, while I laugh and laugh and laugh, real loud.

It would give anybody the creeps to see the fog there is today. I haven't been able to see my hands in front of my face once since day broke, and it's almost noon. It's spooky. This time of year's always this way. But I like it to be this way, anyway. In the fog everything turns white. Celestino and I walk along through that whiteness in the air, bumping into each other, and we hold on to each other so we don't knock our heads off against some big tree trunk. Today is going to be a day with lots of work for Celestino, since he writes more than ever when there's fog; and sometimes night catches us halfway down the mountain, since the scribbling fever doesn't let up on him until everything gets dark and he's stabbed himself in the fingers two or three times

Come,
demon.

— ARTHUR RIMBAUD

with the awl he uses to write with on the trees . . . I like the fog too because this way my old jackass of a grandfather can't find us as easy as when everything is clear and bright, so at least we can breathe easy, thinking we don't have the old man chasing us like a mad dog.

Like always, I've stayed on the path to keep a lookout, except I can't keep a lookout on anything because I can't see anything. Not even myself. I just squint into the big fog that splits open once in a while and then closes right back up again, thicker and whiter than ever. And all I can hear is the sound of the birds singing uncertainly and flying off in lord knows what direction . . . The sound of the birds and Celestino whacking on the trunks of the trees. And I don't worry anymore about how long it might take Celestino to write that poetry. Sometimes I don't want him to ever finish. I wish both of us could die and the poetry could keep going and not ever finish. I think about that because if he finishes one day, I don't know what we would do then, and I wouldn't have any reason to stay about halfway down the road, squatting in the fog and taking care of him. No, I hope he never finishes. Don't rush, real easy. Whack real easy . . . Slow and easy, because real real soon we'll be a couple of little old men and we'll go "poof!" Slow . . . slow . . . slow . . .

Grandpa has finally found us out—I see his hatchet through the fog, glinting and flashing. I yell at Celestino to stop writing and run. The witch takes off running right behind me, too. And the three of us hide in the big rocks that are always just beyond the river . . . The sun, peeking through a little bit now, makes the witch gradually disappear. Adolfina! I call to her, since for a second I see that *she*'s the witch and that she's even looked at me with a little sadness, even. But then she fades away in the whiteness and I'll never know if it was really Adolfina or not . . . You can see Grandpa clearer now than ever, bent over next to the tree trunks Celestino was carving on. The racket of the hatchet is the only thing you can hear now, until Grandpa gets so tired he stretches out on a tree trunk and starts sobbing as loud as he can, almost bawling; you'd think he was literally bellowing . . . Tears start up in Celestino's eyes too and run down his face, and I look up, because maybe it's started to rain and we haven't noticed. If I could, I'd sneak over to where Grandfather was and run my hand across his back, but on second thought the old man is touchy as an old hound, and he'd no more than see me before he'd start growling and snapping. I don't know why that old son of a bitch, that looks like a dried-up little raisin, hates me so much. After all, it's not my fault that Celestino writes poems, and I can't see anything wrong with that anyway. Maybe what the matter with the old man is, is envy. But no, I know he doesn't envy him—what he does is *hate* Celestino and me. Uh-huh, I know it's hate, pure hate, because even now that we're little old men we're still the same age we were when we first came to that house and as he says "we weren't fit to wipe his ass with." Uh-huh, that's what happens—he had the idea that we'd grow up to be the big horse that he is and we just stayed colts. Goddamned old man! don't think for a minute you're going to put shoes on *us!*

Grandpa's hatchet has flown through the air and stuck in Celestino's forehead. I try to pull it out but I can't. Grandpa bursts out laughing and says, "Either you let me brand you or I leave that hatchet right there in the little ninny's face." I don't know what to do, but finally I say okay, I'll let you brand me.

We've come back from the corn planting. Grandpa picked up Celestino and me, and he gave us a ride on his shoulders while we pricked him with our spurs and snapped a whip at him and kicked him. Grandpa didn't say a thing the whole way back and we made him run a lot and then we told him to take us up to the highest part of Dead Man's Hill. So he went up there with us riding him. Then I told him, "Now you have to jump with us on your back from this hill over there to the other one, and if you don't do it I'll pull out your eyes." So Grandpa jumped, but when he came down on the other hill he slipped and fell, with us still on his back. So we tied him up to a naked-boy tree and went "plop" "plop" with the wheel of the spur and popped both his eyes out. He didn't so much as whimper, and I said to him, "Sing," so he sang. Then we got tired of that and we sneaked off without making a sound. My grandfather—my *blind* grandfather—never suspected we had left him there all by himself, so he kept on singing and singing . . . And they say you can still hear the old man singing to this day, walking from one hilltop over to the other and back, and never daring to shut his mouth.

"Don't play with those corncobs. They're to stoke the cook-stove with."

"But these cobs are green."

"I told you to leave those corncobs alone!"

"If I don't play with the corncobs, what am I supposed to play with?"

"With nothing. Dummy! Don't you see you're too old to be such a ninny."

I'm old. They told me, "You're old," so now I'm an old man. From way way up in the Indian laurel tree the little parson birds dive headfirst and peck at me and say, "You're old," "You're old."

I'm old! How wonderful! I'm an old man!

Old!

So old . . . Old. So old . . .

I went to bathe in the creek bed and then I realized I was dreaming and that I wasn't an old man. But when I woke up, Grandma stuck a knife in my throat and said, "Die, old man, what are you waiting for."

Old man . . . I'm an old man! How sad and happy that makes me feel.

They gave me the news last night and at first I didn't want to believe it. I waited for it to be day again, and the sun hadn't come up yet when I ran out to the well and peeked down into it, scared as I could be, to see if it was true that I was an old man. And instead of my wrinkled bony face, what I saw was a little tiny boy swimming with the lignum vitae trees and the shiny green-and-purplish blackbirds and calling me so so pleasantly. But I wasn't scared. I called myself again, but I didn't answer again, and finally I got littler and littler until I got down to the size of an ant, but then I kept shrinking until I lost myself in the bottom and even though I looked and looked down into the well from over the top of the wellhead palings, I couldn't see me . . . I came to the house and started to bawl, standing in the loblolly the water Grandpa throws out from the washbasin makes. My mother ran out of the kitchen so scared, and she asked me—

"Who was it that killed you this time? Tell me, once and for all, who it was that killed you."

"You," said I then to mortify and spite her. "You did, Mama."

She looked at me, and then she began to pray and to beg forgiveness.

"Pay no attention to that hell-bound child," said my grandfather then, coming out of the washhouse with some dirty water to throw into the loblolly. "Pay no attention to that lying hell-bound child, because I was the one that killed him."

My mother calmed down a little then. So we went into her room. My mother's room is so strange. You ought to see it! There is no bed, no window in it. Just a rock, where Mama always has a candle lit that nobody could see a thing by. My mother sleeps stretched out in a corner with a chicken, two roosters and the hens that cover her with droppings all night long, because they climb up on her and roost. Sometimes at night when I run out to the privy I've heard a loud shriek and then all the roosters and the hens cackling and flapping around. I've heard those shrieks and those cackles and flutters and one time, but just one time, I got up the courage to peek in the window, to see what was happening inside. I peeked in the window and I saw my mother hanging from away up on the roof beam and the hens and chickens and roosters jumping and flapping and fluttering, trying to reach the rope tied around my mother's neck—but it was no use. Nobody could jump up to where my mother was hanging, swaying all purple and open-eyed . . . I ran like a streak to my room, where Celestino was in bed and I jumped straight into my bed and lay as still as I could.

"What is it?" said Celestino.

"My mother's hoisted up to the roof beam!"

"What mother?"

"Mine . . ."

"I'll have to wake you up, so you'll realize you're dreaming."

"Uh-huh, wake me up . . ."

But he couldn't. Celestino hit me and hit me again, but nothing happened. I kept on sleeping. And since that time I don't believe I have ever waked up again, because to this day when I go out to the privy at night I hear the scream in my mother's room, and even if many's the time I've wanted to peek in the window, the flapping of the roosters and the hens tells me What for?, because if I do peek in I know I'll see what I saw that one time. So I run back to my room. And I tell myself, Who knows, maybe Celestino can wake me up this night. But he can't; I tell him I'm dreaming and he shakes me as hard as he possibly can. But I keep telling him I'm dreaming.

Grandma and Grandpa have stuffed all the stuff into the big trunk that's out behind the corn press. Then they put a heavy chain around the trunk and make my mother drag it. My mother huffs and tugs, trying to pull it from the front. From the back, Grandpa and Grandma push the trunk. But my grandmother, who you can always trust to be a cunning one, my grandmother clambers up on top of it every few minutes, so my mother has to strain all the harder. They go past the back of the house like that, past the well—where my aunt Adolfina is singing with her mouth closed—and disappear up into the mountain meadow.

I try to catch up with them, but they keep getting farther and farther ahead. They cross the hills near Dogfight and the plains of Clearwater; now they climb the peaks of Gibara . . . As they disappear I keep hearing the hmmmmmm from my aunt Adolfina, and as it keeps getting louder and louder and clearer and clearer it starts sounding so so sad to me, so sad.

I go back to the house, steering myself by that sound.

Adolfina is singing out behind the well, like always, with her mouth closed. She has a great lot of paste of white dirt, water, and lemon stirred up together, and she's covering her whole face with it.

"Adolfina! Adolfina!"

She doesn't answer me. She doesn't stop singing, but she makes herself a new face with her fingers.

"Adolfina!" I scream.

She sticks her fingers into the concoction and makes herself a big huge mouth with a beauty spot just beside it.

"Adolfina! Adolfina!"

She rubs out that face again and makes herself a tiny little itty-bitty mouth, but such big eyes and such big eyebrows that they take up her whole forehead.

I go closer.

"Adolfina," I say, touching her.

Still singing with her mouth closed, she puts on a long straight nose and some mouse ears.

Since she pays me no mind at all, I stick my hands into her face. My fingers sink into the crust of white dirt and it crumbles away and I can see that there's nothing underneath.

"Adolfina! Adolfina!"

But I'm all by myself in a little whitish loblolly, and now it doesn't even make the least little tiny little sound.

Now that everybody has disappeared, and Celestino and I are left in the house all by ourselves, I have started to get so scared. What became of all the people! Where is everybody! Sometimes I stop stock-still in the middle of the road and I wait for somebody to pass by so I can ask what direction the people from my house went off in. But not a soul goes down these roads around here, and when they do pass by they don't pay me the slightest attention. Animals!, every single person that lives in this miserable godforsaken part of the country! I can speak to them as politely as I know how and they still won't acknowledge my existence. So I plant myself in front of the first person that passes by, and I say, "Excuse me, but are you deaf?" But he must be blind too, in that case, because I roll around on the ground and turn somersaults and twist myself into knots so he can see that there's something on my mind. And sometimes I get so mad that I take my fists to the people that pass by (and there are fewer and fewer of them, too), and hit them, but they still don't pay me any mind. So I scream and hop and throw fits, and I throw rocks at the people too. But still so far nobody has ever even looked at me. But that doesn't mean I've given up all hope. I keep waiting and watching—right here, in the middle of the road, sitting on a rock so hard and so uncomfortable, while the great wide silence spreads all across the mountain. I sit here waiting for somebody to pass by, and, even if the person doesn't tell me a word of my family, for him at least to tell me to go to hell—at least for him to do *some*thing.

THE SECOND END

The house is falling down. I sometimes wish I could hold
it up with my hands, but I know it's just falling down
and there's not a thing I can do about it.

I look at this house falling down and I think, That's where
I first met Celestino, and that's where we learned to play hopscotch; I think, That's where my mother first took the strap to
me, and where she put her hand on my head for the first time
and smoothed down my hair. I think, That's the place where one
time Grandpa said "Christmas" and laughed out loud. And it
made me so happy when he said "Christmas" that I don't know
why but I started laughing, and I was so happy and laughing so
hard that I went off to the corner of the breezeway, where the
tulip flowers grow, and over there under the wasp-nest I laughed
and laughed as hard as I could. "Christmas" "Christmas"
"Christmas." And that started me laughing out loud all over
again, so hard I didn't even feel the wasps that were already
buzzing and swarming around my ears. "Christmas" "Christmas" "Christmas."

And I rolled around and writhed all over the floor, I was so
happy.

And now the house is falling down. If it does finally fall
down, what'll become of those voices I still hear saying "Christmas" "Christmas" over and over again. What'll become of me,
still rolling around from being so happy, over there in the breeze-

way under the wasp-nest. If the house falls down, the water closet and the crocks will smash into a million pieces, and then I'm not going to be able to keep on living. If the house falls down, the big old cookstove, that's just slapped together out of wet ashes, will crumble to pieces too, and then I'm not going to be able to keep on living. If the house falls down all the jabbering and carrying-on of my cousins, who come to the Christmas Eve party, would come tumbling down too, and I'm not going to be able to keep on living. And the worst thing of all—if the house does finally fall down, we'd have to move away into another one, and then I'd have to start being born all over again, and find another word all over again to make me laugh out loud like that. And convince the wasps all over again to put up a wasp-nest in the breezeway. And keep after Grandpa all over again to pour some water into the washtub in the yard and to make a loblolly like the one there is now. And I'd have to wait for a long long long time for the roof to get black from the smoke and soot, like the one on our house is now, and maybe it wouldn't even get the way this one is if you waited a long time. And if the house doesn't have an old smoky black roof I don't want to live in it. And if the house doesn't have cracks in it all over the place and you can't see the same thing through every single crack that I can see through these ones, I don't want to live in it. And if the house doesn't have some goat's feet, up next to some ears of corn strung up, hanging from the ridgepole of the roof, I don't want to live in it, either. And if the house doesn't have a corner door and if there's not an old termite-eaten piece of palm thatch leaning up next to the corner door, I don't want to live in it. And even if it does have all those things—if the house doesn't have a well, full of maidenhair ferns and voices, then I'll never ever live in it . . . No, there couldn't ever be another house that would be like this one and hide all the secret things I've done in it. The other one would be strange for me, and I'd be strange for it, too.

So then I cry, because I know the house doesn't exist anymore. But as soon as I start crying I stop again, because I remember I'll have to move away into a new house and there's no way it'll know about this crying. So I'm just wasting my time.

We were coming back from picking star apples when Mama stopped stock-still at the highest spot in the orchard and said—

"The house is getting to be so ugly! It looks like it's about to collapse and fall down." And she broke out laughing.

I threw the star apples down on the ground and started bawling.

"But, child, don't be silly," she said all soft and loving, my mother, while she was laughing. "Can't you see that what I'm telling you is just foolishness, it's got nothing to do with anything?"

So we went into the house, me drying my eyes on the hem of Mama's slip, since she had the skirt tucked up into her waist so the skirt tail was doubled up into a kind of basket, full of star apples.

The house is lying flat on the ground, so we pick up the boards and the leaves of palm thatch and set them, one by one, the same place they were in before. We tie the husks of the palm branches all over again with strips stripped right off the husks, so they're held in place like before. All of us work at putting the house back together again. I direct the work. Sometimes I pick up the broomstick and give a whack or two. One whack for my mother, across her shoulders, because she's such a poor slow worker. Another whack on my grandmother's head every time she straightens up to catch her breath. And one last whack, harder than the other ones, for the old man, who's on top of the roof, because he's not tying down the palm husks tight at all, and that might mean that one of these days the house might fall down again. So that's why my grandfather always gets the biggest whack.

Celestino got up at midnight and he hasn't come back. I saw him get up in the dark and I called him real soft so Grandpa wouldn't find out that he was sleeping in the house. But he didn't answer me. He jumped out the window and disappeared into the first patches of fog. The fog is starting to rise so early these days! It must be because the cold months are here; but really, it never gets *cold* cold—winter comes and is over and then comes back again, and we go right on frying to a crisp. I started to follow Celestino, but when I tried to get out of bed the witch came in and she squeezed my hand and she said, *"There" "There"* "Go, write whatever you want to on the tree trunks." That's exactly what the witch told me, and with that I got sleepier and sleepier and sleepier, even if I didn't want to. But as hard as I tried to make sleep go away, I couldn't manage to do it, and I kept yawning and yawning, until I saw the witch fading out right before my eyes and I said to myself, Now I'm asleep.

Now, with it noon already and Celestino not back yet, I don't know what to do. Mama's asked me about him but I haven't dared tell her the truth, because I can't trust my mother, I figure she'll tattle on Celestino to my grandfather and he'll go to where Celestino is writing and give him a whack with the hatchet in his back. So I don't say a thing to my mother—though you don't have to tell her things for her to know them, she notices everything. All I have to do is look at her and I know that just *that* fast she's figured out what I didn't tell her. She really is that way. I still remember the time she was telling me a story and she started crying, so I asked her what she was crying about and she told me, "I just don't understand why you want me to die. Am I that mean to you?" I didn't know what to say. But she told me that if I was thinking about her dying it wasn't because I wanted her to die, it was because if she did then I'd get to bawl and everybody would come and listen to me.

"Where are you going?" the witch said.
"To look for Celestino."
"Why don't you just stay still."
"No. I want to tell him Grandpa's on his way with the hatchet to cut off his head."
"You know that, so he does too."

ELEKTRA: Then where is
   the tomb of that wretch?

ORESTES: There is no
   such tomb. He that lives
   has no need of it.

   — Sophocles

Grandpa goes up and buries the hatchet in Celestino's head. Celestino doesn't yell, he doesn't make a sound. Not a peep. He just goes right on writing something on the tree trunk, with the hatchet splitting his head open and everything, and then he dances a little with the chorus of dead cousins that appears all of a sudden under the branches of a breakax tree. The cousins start singing to him so he'll keep dancing. But he doesn't. He goes off walking for a while and he walks all over the mountain. He comes to the high mountain meadow and from there he looks around at everything. And that's when he sees me, just coming out of the house, going to warn him about what it's already too late for. Then he sits down on a rock and picks up a stick and (with that one-track mind of his) he starts to write in the dirt. But the ground is too dry. It's so dry that finally he gives up and lies down on it. And people say that by the time they got there he was already dead.

And people say that by the time they got there he was already dead.

He was dead.
He was dead.
He was dead.

People don't know what they're talking about.
I came to where he was lying and I said to him—
"Does it hurt a lot where they hit you with the hatchet?"
"What hatchet?" he said. And we started to talk like we always did—not saying a word.

That night I helped Celestino up and slowly we walked to the house.
"This is the house," I said.
"The house . . . ," he said.
The witch was crying when she came to the parlor door to let us in.

"I told you so!" the witch said. "I told you so!" And she hugged me and bawled a lot, real real softly, and finally she disappeared into thin air.

Celestino and I went into the parlor. There was my mother dead.

"Your mother died," said the chorus of cousins.

"What mother? . . ."

"*Your* mother, the one that watered the bileweed plants and said they were coleus."

"Well, what about the other one?"

"The other one jumped in the well a long time ago."

"So which ones do we have left?"

"We don't know. But one mother or another may still be left for you around here somewhere scattered around."

"Tell them there's no use their coming around now anymore."

The parlor is full of people.

The chorus of cousins disappears.

My mother is flickering and flashing in the four candles burning real real slowly.

Come closer! Come closer! Your mother is flickering and flashing in the four candles burning real real slowly.

Come closer! Come closer! Here is your mother. Such sweet sleep. Finally. Finally you are the center of all the attention.

Closer!

Closer!

The chorus of cousins comes down off the roof, and they all cry for you. Everybody here wipes their eyes, for you.

Closer!

Taking one slow step at a time, I step slowly closer. My mother is waiting for me, so peacefully now, inside the coffin that my grandmother says is made out of cedar, and that's why it cost so much.

"This coffin is made out of cedar?"

"Uh-huh, cedar."

"And it cost a whole lot?"

"A whole whole lot."

"How much?"

"An arm and a leg."

"Whose?"

"Your grandfather's."

"Poor Grandpa, he must have thrown a fit!"

"A fit nothing! He went into such a state that to this minute he hasn't come out of the privy."

Closer!

Your mother is waiting for you in that big box. Finally, for once in your life, you will have your day in the limelight. This is your night. These people are yours. Your mother is yours. The time is yours.

Closer!

All of it is yours. Those faces cry for you, and they feel for you, and they pity you. Even your grandmother, that has always hated you so much, has asked about you, how you were. "How's the wart?" she said, and she tried to make her growly muttering sound nasty, but she couldn't manage that . . . This is your big day! This is your big day!

Closer!

From Dogfight, from Lignum Vitae, from Big Filly, from Admiral's Rest, from Kettletown, from Kenneltown, from Lariat, from Buzzard, from Clearwater—from towns and villages for miles around people have come just to see you cry. *Cry*, don't let this opportunity go to waste. The audience has assembled. They are packed in shoulder to shoulder to see you. You, only you. You are all there is. Come closer to this big box waiting for you in the flickering lights!

Closer!

This is your greatest moment. Everyone's eyes are glued to you.

Walk slowly, learn to enjoy this moment reserved for you. Slowly. Savor the moment. Savor it. Sa—vo—rrr it.

Closer!

Slowly. Give them the chance to hear you cry. Give them the chance to feel sorry for you. So they'll finally say "Poor thing." They're starting to love you already. They aren't crying for her now, they're crying for you. They would like to be your mother now.

They adore you now.
Enjoy it.
    I enjoy it.
Cry.
    I'm crying.
Bawl.
    I'm bawling.
Throw your arms around the coffin.
    I throw my arms around the coffin.
Say "Mother, Mother, don't leave me here all alone."
    "Mother, Mother, don't leave me here all alone!"
Now cry harder.
    I cry harder.
Scream.
    Aaaaaagh!
Throw yourself on the floor, but don't give the people time to
come pick you up, stand up yourself before they can get to you,
and say, "Leave me alone, leave me alone with her."
    "Leave me alone, leave me alone with her."
But don't let them leave you alone, because then . . .
    "Don't leave me alone! Don't leave me alone!"
Now you are standing in front of the coffin.
    Now I'm standing in front of the coffin.
Say, softly and slowly, "My mother!"
    "My mother . . ."
"You've gone and left me here alone."
    "You've gone and left me here all alone."
"Now who is there left to carry water for in the afternoons."
    "Now who is there left to carry water for in the afternoons."
Fall asleep, still clutching the coffin.
    Now I'm asleep.
Your time is up, we better get back to the cornfield.
    My time is up, I better get back to the cornfield.

Today we went for a walk, and when we were coming back
Grandma showed me how to pick out the Big Dipper, the Plow-
man, and the Swan. Celestino already knew all about the sky
and without Grandma telling him he picked out the Milky Way.

146

All writing points beyond earthly limits.

—FATHER CHARLES

Grandma said she was going to carry me a while because it looked like I was worn out. So she carried me. But in a little while she was the one that started to wear out. So she put me down and told me, "Give me your hand. I don't want you stumbling into some tree stump." And we went on walking. Coming up to the house I did stumble into a tree stump, and it went right through me, into my stomach. Grandma pulled the stump out of my stomach. But I was already dead.

"It was all my fault," said my grandmother then, pulling herself up as tall as she could. "It's all my doing because I didn't carry him right on to the house!"

"Don't be a ninny!" my grandfather told her. "Why is it your fault if that rattlebrain doesn't know how to put one foot in front of the other!"

My mother let out a wail and ran out of her room.

"All I had left, you damned jackasses!" she said, yanking me out of my grandmother's arms and holding me.

"Now what is there left to live for!" she said again and ran with me dead in her arms out into the yard.

The yard was full of a heavy heavy fog. Celestino was in the fog and he smiled at me when he saw me go by in my mother's arms. "Tonight we'll burn some spiders," I heard him say to me, grinning like an imp, but I didn't say a thing to him, because I was scared Mama would hear me and suspect he was around someplace.

"Okay," I told Celestino two or three weeks after that night, because my mother was still carrying me around in her arms till then. She had walked the mountain over like she was crazy, but she had finally come back to the house half naked and her feet cut to ribbons and put me down.

Finally Christmas Eve is almost here and all my cousins have come, practically gasping for breath from the load of aunts they've had to drag along with them. My aunts are a loud bunch. They screech at each other and fight like dogs and cats. But not my cousins—they're not that way, except according to my aunts my cousins never stop mortifying and spiting them, to make their lives miserable. There are eleven of my aunts and more than fifty of my cousins . . . What a mess of people in the house, madre mía! What a mess of people! This is going to be quite a Christmas Eve. The pigs are almost spitted already, and we're all playing and singing in the arbor that's absolutely full of green soursops and fire ants like red-hot pokers. It would be so nice if it were always Christmas Eve! My cousins would be at our house all year long. And I could play with them anytime I wanted to. We'd always be playing Simon Says or hopscotch or hide-and-seek. Or just playing. But anyway they'd always be here with me. I wish they wouldn't ever have to leave! . . . The chorus of boy cousins goes over to the chorus of girl cousins and they make a circle, boy-girl, boy-girl, and one girl gets in the middle. Then they all start singing.

> Sally, Sally Wallflower, come sprinkle your plants,
> For down in the meadow there lies a young man.
> Rise, Sally, rise, and don't you look sad,
> For you shall have a husband, good or bad.
> Choose you one, choose you two,
> Choose the nicest you can see!

> *The nicest one that I can see*
> *Is that one* there, *please come to me!*

> Now you are married, I wish you good joy,
> First a girl, and then a boy;
> Seven years now and seven to come,
> Take her and kiss her, and send her off home.

Then another one's It.

We've been out horseback riding all afternoon on great big horses made out of crepe myrtle trunks. Poor horses, they must be worn out! We better take them to the pasture.

Celestino and I gallop off on the stick horses and tie them

up in the acacias so they can't run away, because these horses are not broken yet, and if you don't tie them up good they'll take off like the devil was after them. Damned jackasses!

Your girl cousins have built a house out of boards up in the very top of the cherry tree. They're playing. How pretty your cousins look up in the top of the big cherry tree that looks like it's going to buckle under from all that weight. Look at them! Look at them up there playing house. Now they're lighting the woodstove. Look at them! Look at them playing on the big board for the floor, and those old tables they've put way way up there in the highest branches. They say the house is a house built with a lot of stories in it. And it's true. How high and pretty your cousins' playhouse is! Where they sing and fight and sweep and cook. Look at them! Look at them! Today looks like the day to pay visits, because they're all in the same place talking and talking and talking. They talk about their daughters and about what kind of sickness one of their dolls came down with when she drank a glass of chameleon milk. About the measles going around. They think bees are spirits, so when one of them flies by to suck at the cherry flowers, the girls shoo it off and move their lips like they were really and truly praying. Look! Look at your cousins up there playing house! They talk and talk and talk, and one of them has put coffee on and another one has tied a sack from one branch to another and is rocking her doll, but it doesn't look like it wants to go to sleep. Will you have to climb all the way up to the top of the cherry tree and give it four whacks on its fanny? You're that infant's father, and it's up to you to teach it to behave. But no . . . but you're dying to climb up there, aren't you? But you can't do it. Resign yourself to looking at them from down on the ground; you're not a girl. *"You're a little man and you shouldn't always be playing with the girls."* . . . You are a little man . . .

You ninny! Off with the girls again!

.   .   .

The doll keeps crying and kicking, and then she kicks so hard it rocks the hammock and she rolls out, and she bounces down from one branch to another and lands on the ground, which is covered with chicken droppings because the hens sleep in that cherry tree too. You run towards the doll lying there and don't even bother about getting chicken shit all over your hands, you snatch her up on the run and take off. You run with her, shit all over her, and go hide, out behind the stand of prickly-leafed wild pineapples.

Now you rock her and kiss her. And when you kiss her your lips get chicken droppings all over them. But who's close enough to you to take the strap and put you over their knee? *Nobody.* Nobody's watching. You can do whatever you downright feel like doing. Nobody's looking at you. This is your chance.

Those women don't know how to take care of you like I do . . . There! Hush! . . . Be still . . . Be still. You're with me all safe out here behind the wild pineapple thicket. There . . . nobody's going to spank you! Stay here with me, don't pay any attention to those sissy girls . . . Now you're here all by yourself with me! Don't cry! Don't cry! I'm rocking you now . . . I'm rocking you now! . . .

Rock her. Rock her.

"Here now, hush, we don't want the boys to find us! We don't want them to find out I'm doing dirty things with a little rag doll. Hush! Hush! Don't cry . . ."

Now they're hunting for me. Here they come! I better hurry up.

Hurry up! Hurry up!

They're getting closer! If they catch me doing this with a doll, they'll throw rocks at me and beat me up.

. . .

They're getting closer, and if they catch you doing that with a doll they're going to throw rocks at you and beat you up. Button up your pants, they're right over there. Let it go for another day. Young man, behave yourself. Here come the people . . .

There, now . . . Don't cry, I'll rock you. Don't cry; nobody's watching us. That zzzzooop was a lizard. Those damned jackass lizards hate my guts—all they do is pester me! But don't pay any mind to them, they're just a bunch of lizards. There, now! There now! We're almost finished. They're just lizards! Lizards! Be still! . . . Lizards! . . . Lizards! . . .

There come the boys, with your grandfather heading up the pack. Here they come. Now they've seen you. They've caught you at that filthiness! So what if you've finished—they saw you. Run, before they catch you. Run! You don't even have time to pull up your pants. Run! Run!

All my cousins have seen me. How embarrassing! I wish I could crawl in a hole. How will I ever look them in the face when I'm playing with them and we go off over there to throw rocks at the birds. How embarrassing! . . . Even my mother heard the story, and she comes running up to me with my pants all hitched up and twisted and the doll looking like something that had been through the grinder.

You beast! You beast!
That's your grandmother. What a squawk she sets up. Old she-goat biddy, she's so put out with you she doesn't want to see your face. Every time I go in the kitchen she throws scalding water on me, and one day she almost cracked my skull with that rock you mash up garlic with. Ugly old she-goat! I hate you till I can't hate you anymore!

"Pig!" . . . The other day she wrung my favorite hen's neck—
the hen that laid an egg every single afternoon.

"What you did is disgusting! You ought to be ashamed. You're
not a little boy anymore."

*You half-wit! Just wait till I catch you. I'm going to geld
you once and for all!*

Listen to that. That's your grandfather. He's one of the goody-
goodies too. I hate that old so-and-so. As though he wasn't the
one that had taught me how to do those things! Uh-huh, it was
him—he always took the fillies down to the river to wash them
and when he was through washing them he'd have me hold them
by the bit while he fooled with them and fooled with them again
from the back.

Grab him! Grab him!

Listen to my cousins. My damned self-righteous cousins. But
they do dirty things too, I'll have you know, just like me, and
one time they killed a poor nanny goat . . . But never mind that.
I can't face them with that. I can't face anybody anymore—because everybody has found out about it. It's so embarrassing. Of
course they always did it so there was no way for anybody to
know about it. But I feel like dying. Everybody knows about it
now, so Celestino probably even knows about it now too—him,
that's never done any of those nasty things. How embarrassing!
How embarrassing! I'd be better off gelded once and for all so
these fits wouldn't ever come over me anymore. That's what I
ought to do. As soon as I get the chance I'm going to sharpen the
butcher knife on the grindstone and I'm going to cut them off.
That's what you'll do. That's what you'll do. Here they come,
running after you, they've almost caught you. Run! Run!

"You old so-and-so, you're not going to whack *me* with that
hatchet!"

"Stop right there, you damned little son of a bitch! Don't
think you can get away from *me.*"

"Catch him!"

"He's the one that wrung my hen's neck!"

"He's getting away!"

"My God, he's running off naked! How embarrassing!"

"Rope him!"

"Young man, you might skin your balls that way!"

"You damned old jackass! You'll never see hide nor hair of me again!"

"I hope you die!"

"Monster!"

"Stupid!"

"Young man! Pull up your pants this minute before you fall and skin yourself!"

"Sic the dogs on him!"

"Just let him go! If he gets onto the highway they'll take him to jail!"

"You're not going to catch me! You'll never catch me!"

"I think the very devil's got into him. Look at what he did to this doll . . ."

"My lord!"

"Ay! and you didn't see that pretty hen that laid an egg as regular as clockwork!"

"Holy Mary full of grace, the Lord is with thee. Blessed be the fruit of thy womb. Holy Mary, mother of God. Mother of God, mother of God, mother of God . . ."

"What's wrong?"

"There are some pages missing out of this prayer book."

"*Virgen santísima!* Who could've done such a thing!"

"I know who it was."

"Who?"

"I'm not telling."

"Tell me! Unless you want me to slap you into next Christmas!"

"Who told you you could tear the pages out of the prayer book?"

"I didn't know it had prayers in it."

"You ought to be cudgeled till you're dead! Just look at what you've put us through, look at the shame of it—we invite To-masico's wife over here—the only soul for miles around that knows how to read—we have to go get her on a horse and give her two turkeys so she'll come read the novena for your mother, and you go and do this! You ought to be beat to death!"

"It's all his cousin's fault—ever since he set foot in this house he hasn't done a thing but teach him one kind of filthiness after another."

"Liar!"

"How dare you call your grandmother a liar! I'll teach you!"

WHACK!

"Liar!"

"Again?!"

WHACK!

"Celestino hasn't taught me anything! I knew it all from before!"

"Shut your mouth if you don't want me to shut it for you . . . I thought I'd die of mortification when I saw that that good-for-nothing little ninny had covered the tree trunks with dirty words. And now your grandfather can barely get around, from the pain he got in his kidneys from spending all day cutting down the trees that fool scribbled and cut all over . . ."

"That's not true! What he wrote is poetry . . ."

"Poetry my sweet tit!"

"Poetry—that's what he told me it was!"

"And you believe everything that shameless do-nothing tells you! He's his father's son all right. Just like a Pupo! I swear, I told your grandfather when that pervert father of his came to ask for Carmelina's hand. I told him, I said, 'That man is good for nothing.' But no—to get her off his hands, he said he could have her. And this is the upshot of it—a dirty, filthy, stinking child that doesn't work worth beans, that the only thing he does is write filth on the trees. And one of these days we'll all be keeling over from the heat because pretty soon there won't be a tree left standing in the whole yard that your grandfather hasn't had to cut down. Oh, I could just die from shame when I think that somebody that knows how to read might come by here and see some of that filth written on the trees! What in the world will they think of us! . . ."

I am he who,
incessantly,
I make myself.

— Tristan Corbière

"How do *you* know what he writes, if you don't know how to read yourself?"

"I may not know how, but Tomasico's wife does—and when we took her and showed her the tree trunks that Celestino had scribbled all over, thinking the poor little thing was writing his poor dead mother's name—why, the name of his dead mother, nothing! He doesn't even remember who his mother was. Yessir, I mean it—and if I remember correctly one of the things Tomasico's wife read went 'Who will be my mother,' 'Who will be my mother,' 'for I look for her in the privy but I don't see her' . . . You tell *me*—a woman not eight days dead, and he doesn't even remember who she was! And then to say he went looking for her in the outhouse! That just about beats everything! Looking for a woman in an outhouse! Like she was a turd!"

The whacks of the hatchet chopping is clearer now. You can catch a glimpse of the shape of tiny, old, old Celestino once in a while now, not much more than a shadow among the big tree trunks, writing and writing and never stopping for a second. I go up closer and look at him a minute. But right away I drop my eyes and I sit down on the path to keep a lookout. And I prick up my ears and realize the chopping of the hatchet is getting closer and closer.

Celestino doesn't hear a thing. He hasn't rested day or night for a week now, and he hasn't eaten a bite. I run to the house and steal something to eat from Grandma and carry it to him. But he ignores me completely. He just keeps writing and writing and writing like a crazy person, so I say to myself, "It's just not possible that those are bad words he's putting there. It can't be— he's writing something so pretty, he must be, but that old she- ass wife of Tomasico's, she doesn't understand, nor me either, and that's why she says it's filth. They're a bunch of savages! If they don't understand something, they automatically hate it. They say it's ugly or it's dirty. Animals! . . . I wish I could at least learn to write that word—*Animals*. I wish I could learn hen- scratching. I wish somebody would teach me . . . That's the only thing I'd want to know, so I could start putting it on all the tree trunks, and even on the branches of the guava trees, and even on the ceiba tree, that's got all those thorns. I'd put "Animals" on every one of them. Till there wasn't a tree left that didn't have that word scratched into it. And it would drive that old so-and-so of a grandfather of mine crazy, cutting down one tree after another after another. And every time he went to cut one down, the first thing he'd see would be the word "Animals." And he'd keep cutting them down and the trees would keep saying *Animals*, till he couldn't take it anymore and he'd fall down dead on the ground, from exhaustion . . . But no, that wouldn't work, because that thick-skulled grandpa of mine is such a goddamned jackass and a mule that he doesn't even know how to make a circle for an *O*. But I don't either . . . But it doesn't matter whether I understand what Celestino is writing or not. I know it's something beautiful, because if it was really ugly like they say it is, *that* wouldn't bother my family one bit, and they wouldn't keep pestering him so.

"There's Grandpa coming like a mad dog! Let's run!"
"Which way?"
"That way."
"But that's the way he's coming."
"Then let's go this way."
"He's over there too."
"Let's run around that corner over there!"
"He's coming around that corner."
"Let's fly!"
"Look—he's up there in the clouds, holding his hatchet up ready for us."
"What do we do!"
"Let's see if we can talk him out of it."
"But *how?*"

Grandma and Grandpa have taken us down to the river.
But they didn't want to go swimming.
I asked them why they didn't go in and go swimming and they told me they were too old for that kind of thing, for us to go ahead in and go swimming.

So I jumped in the water.

And I was swimming with my cousins.

There were so many of us we barely fit in the river. And I dived under and swam over to where Celestino was and I pushed him into the deep hole.

Celestino was drowning. But I ran and saved him.

"Don't let me drown," he was saying, and he grabbed me around the neck. "Don't let me drown!"

So we swam to the bank.

Then I laid him down in the grass and I went off with the rest of my cousins.

"What's the matter with Celestino?" Grandma said.

"He was drowning and I saved him," I said.

"Such boys. They're always playing like they're drowning!"

I've sat up all night long. Celestino doesn't feel so good. But he doesn't want to say anything. But I know he's sick anyway. The sheets are like boilerplate, his fever is so high, and they're wringing wet like somebody had wet the bed, he's sweat so much.

"You're dying."

"What foolishness! . . ."

"You want me to make you some wormseed tea, in case it's a belly worm?"

"No."

"What do you want?"

"Nothing. I'm remembering what January told me."

"Madre mía!"

"You're starting to remember too, aren't you?"

"I can almost remember . . . But the exact word won't come to me."

Finally Christmas Eve has gotten here. I get up bright and early and make a lot of noise so everybody will wake up. My cousins are jabbering and carrying on like jay birds. My aunts scream at them at the top of their lungs. They don't know what to do—all us boys are running around all over and jumping from one bed to another, yelling and carrying on and throwing things at each other's heads. Grandma is ready to spit fire because Grandpa is drunk and he doesn't want to kill the pigs.

"I'm the one that's always got to do everything that gets done in this place! I'm nothing but a slave in this house! The only thing that old coot knows how to do worth doing is get drunk, *period!*"

"What about your period?" one of my aunts pipes up, and they all laugh. Old Jezebels . . .

Madre mía, what a hullabaloo. I'm so happy. I run out to the yard and climb up in the ceiba tree in one jump . . . There's Celestino in his nest. "Today is Christmas Eve," I tell him. "Aren't you glad?" "Uh-huh, I'm awfully glad," he says. But it looks to me like he's awfully sad. "You're not planning to get out of the nest today." "Uh-uh, I'm not going to get out, because the wild dove hasn't come back all night and I have to stay here and keep the eggs warm." . . . That made me as serious as I could be too for a minute; but then I skip up, break out laughing, and climb up on a cloud and tell Celestino, "Okay, then, I'll tell you how the party's going and bring you some candy and all."

The pigs are on the spits. Grandma roasts all three at the same time because Grandpa hasn't been able to set foot out of bed (although if you ask me I think he jumped out the window and took to the mountain) and my aunts and cousins are dancing in the parlor. My mother is so pretty! She's dancing in the parlor too. My mother is so pretty today! She's taken off that stiff black dress she's always harnessed into and put on a dress with great big flowers that look like croton leaves, and she's dancing while a bunch of my cousins beat on the seat of a stool and sing happy songs. Celestino flies down out of the nest once in a while and flutters over to where I am. I'm the only one that sees him come in, but then he turns around all of a sudden and flies off again, very straight-faced, and I get a little worried. But the party is so big and nice and the racket is so loud and there's so much laughing and carrying on that I almost forget about Celestino; so it's only when I see him come through the air, real real quiet, and light on one of my shoulders, that I remember that he exists and that he's way way up there in the thorns of the ceiba tree, warming some eggs that aren't even his own . . . Finally Grandma takes the pigs off the spits and puts them on a big palm leaf. We all make a rush at them, but Grandma picks up a stick and beats us back and says—

"Get in line, unless you want me to skin you all!"

My aunts stop dancing. How funny! All my aunts dance by themselves because not a one of them has got a husband. It's that there's not a man that can stand up to them, and the few of them that did ever get married, it was a pure miracle—but as soon as their husbands saw what kind of woman they'd let themselves in for, they disappeared without a trace . . . Although to hear my grandmother tell it, my aunts were unhusbanded by a hex Toña the washwoman put on them. She was always in love with my grandfather, so my grandmother had her drink some coffee she'd put a spell on. And the woman kicked the bucket. But before she died she said, "This spell you put on me will pass to your daughters now, you wicked old she-goat." And it looks like that's exactly what it did, too, to judge by the fact that not a one of them ever got much past the church door, or that if they did the vows didn't take. Why, hardly anybody ever even looked at them a second time.

Now everyone is sitting at the table. Now they serve you the food. Your mother loves you very much, she tries to find you the best pieces. But you shouldn't eat so much. Remember, today is the Big Day.

Now everyone is sitting at the table. The Big Day has finally arrived.

The chorus of aunts enters, in rags.

The elves enter, a small group at a time. And your dead cousins glow like the morning. They take the same form they always take.

Your mother enters, from the kitchen, grumbling, and says:

MOTHER: He ate the whole roast pig.

So Grandma, who has drunk too much red wine, eats a hunk of boiled plantain and spits on the ground every time she looks at you.

Seconds before the witches enter, Grandfather enters carrying a dead bird.

GRANDMOTHER (*to Grandfather*):   You old drunk! Where have you been! You idle jackass! I've had to do everything in this house all by myself. But you, you half-brained old coot, you're out there somewhere bird hunting...

GRANDFATHER: I may be drunk, but that doesn't mean I've lost my aim. And tonight I'm gonna show you...

GRANDMOTHER: Pig!

GRANDFATHER: Yessir, good aim. Look here, I went out to look at the ceiba tree, to see if that fool Celestino had put something indecent on it, and look what I brought back—a bird like you don't see many of! Just look at those colors!

YOU: Let me see it!

GRANDFATHER: Get back there, you runt of a little monkey! You've always got shit all over your hands.

GRANDMOTHER: You're worse than a child. Imagine going out bird hunting today of all days, with all the work there is to be done in this house!

GRANDFATHER: I tell you I didn't go out hunting *anything*. I just saw it up in the nest and I threw a rock at it to chase it off and it fell over dead and dropped on the ground.

YOU: Let me see it!

CHORUS OF AUNTS: What a stubborn child! How in the world can he be so stubborn!... Why should he want to see that bird so bad? Be still unless you want us to smack you, since that cow of a mother of yours never lays a finger on you. Ah, but it will be a different story with us. Don't think you're going to get away with being a shiftless pervert like your father!

MOTHER: The first one killed!

GRANDMOTHER: Hush, you uncivilized slut! How can you talk like that; can't you see he's listening!

CHORUS OF AUNTS (*to Grandmother*):   She was right, what she said. How could there be anything worse than having a pervert for a son! Not death itself is worse!

GRANDMOTHER: Bitches!

CHORUS OF DEAD COUSINS: How very very sad—I went fishing down at the creek bed and I didn't catch so much as a crawfish. On the road coming back I didn't know what to do, and all of a sudden it got to be night. So I sat down on a rock and I cried. But nobody came along and said "What's the matter."

THE WITCHES (*coming into the parlor*): Nobody came along and said "What's the matter."

CHORUS OF DEAD COUSINS: The well is the only one that knows I'm sad today. You ought to have seen how it cried too, beside me. But that didn't make me feel one tiny bit better, because I know the well is me, so that's why it listens to me—but then again, that means that *nobody* listens to me . . . All night long, and I couldn't find a living soul to talk to, just dead people and trees. So then what else could I do but start carving on them, so at least that way they would know a *little* bit of it.

THE WITCHES: Know a *little* bit of it . . .

CHORUS OF DEAD COUSINS: But I'm so stupid. I don't know how to write. So now I'm thinking I may have written something stupid, or spelled it wrong. But no matter whether I wrote it right or not, I still feel better. I got to the house at sunrise, and there he was, asleep. Who could he be? I've never spoken to him. I've never said the first word to him. But he's always there, already asleep. Waiting for me—because I know he'd been waiting for me. And since I took so long getting back, he finally fell asleep. But asleep and all, I know he had been waiting for me.

THE WITCHES: Had been waiting for me . . .

CHORUS OF DEAD COUSINS: But I'm afraid to wake him up, because I don't know . . . maybe he was waiting for me so he could kill me.

AN ELF: If you look into my eyes, you will fall down dead!

ANOTHER ELF: Fall down dead!

CHORUS OF ELVES: Look into my eyes! Wake me up and look at me!

(*All eat. The meal goes on uninterruptedly as the conversation continues.*)

CHORUS OF AUNTS (*to you, and chewing all the while*):   You're pale, you're sad.

YOU: No.

CHORUS OF AUNTS: Yes, you can see it in your eyes. You're sick. Your mother should put you to bed.

YOU: Leave me alone.

CHORUS OF AUNTS: You are dying! . . . Finally! He's finally dying!

GRANDFATHER: If you look in this bird's eyes, you will fall down dead!

MOTHER (*touching you over the table*):   It's true, you have a fever. (*She stands up and lets out a wail.*) My son is dying!

GRANDFATHER: If you close your eyes you'll see the bird looking at you!

MOTHER: Dying!

GRANDFATHER: If you open your eyes you'll see the bird looking at you!

MOTHER: Dying . . .

CHORUS OF AUNTS: Bring a candle! Bring a candle! Finally!

MOTHER: My God!

YOU: Show me the bird! Show me the bird!

GRANDFATHER (*very cheerfully*):   Here it is! Look at it!

YOU: Celestino!

GRANDFATHER: Yes, you!

MOTHER: Dying . . .

CHORUS OF AUNTS: At last! At last! And it's only right that we should be happy—now he is free. Here the unfortunate ones are us. Us, the victims, daughters of that old drunk and that crazy old crone.

GRANDMOTHER (*who has never stopped eating*):   Evil sluts! Damn you all! (*Goes on eating.*)

CHORUS OF AUNTS: Yes, damned. You at least had the chance to give birth many many times. How many happy nights does each and every one of us represent? How many nights? A hundred?

For whom
has Nature
adorned herself
this year?

— Pan Yuan Tche

GRANDFATHER (*leering*):   Oh, more, more . . .

CHORUS OF AUNTS: Two hundred seventy? Two hundred and seventy, yes, exactly. Two hundred seventy nights of tumbling and struggling and heavy breathing for every miserable one of us.

GRANDFATHER: Exactly! Exactly! And sometimes more.

GRANDMOTHER (*interrupting her meal*):   Damn you!

CHORUS OF AUNTS: For fifty years or more we will face hunger. We will eat dirt. We will live without a man, because that pair of old coots felt like having their fun every night.

GRANDMOTHER: Damn you all!

CHORUS OF AUNTS: And damn you! Damn us all!

GRANDMOTHER (*to Grandfather*):   That's always the way Christmas Eves wind up around here. Ay, my God, what great tragedy this house has seen. Instead of giving birth to human beings I've given birth to savage beasts. We can't even be decent and eat together like human beings one day out of the year. Wild beasts! You are the ones that are damned! What fault is it of mine if you haven't found anybody to go to bed with. I found mine! Look at him, right there! (*Points to Grandfather.*)

GRANDFATHER (*holding up the dead bird*):   Here I am!

GRANDMOTHER: That is the father of you children, fight with him too, I didn't bring you into the world all by myself. And if I had, I'd have brought better, not the garbage your father always made . . . because he doesn't know how to do anything right. A good husband—that's what I've always needed!

GRANDFATHER: Praise the Lord!

GRANDMOTHER: A good husband!

CHORUS OF AUNTS: A good husband! A good husband! (*Some dance with others, and Grandfather and Grandmother also dance.*) A good husband! (*Grandfather throws the dead bird on the table and goes on dancing.*)

MOTHER (*shouting*):   He's dead! He's dead!

(*You get up and make your way through the crowd of cousins, elves, and witches.*)

CHORUS OF DEAD COUSINS (*halting*):   Don't come this way if you haven't kept your word! The promise you made us! (*They repulse him.*)

YOU: Now I am dead.

AN ELF: Come back to life.

YOU: How?

ALL THE ELVES: I don't know!

A WITCH: Let's see . . .

ALL THE WITCHES: Let us see . . .

A DEAD COUSIN (*crying*):   Celestino! Celestino! How dare you come with empty hands! . . .

YOU: They killed me before my time.

MOTHER (*coming up to you and running her hand over you and crying*):   Ay, my son! The only thing I had left in the world! What will become of me now! (*Stops crying and goes on dancing, to the tune of raucous music, just as the Aunts, Grandfather, and Grandmother are dancing.*)

THE WITCHES: Don't cry, there is still something that must be done.

YOU: What can I do, if I'm already dead.

A WITCH: Come back to life!

YOU: They'll kill me again.

A DEAD COUSIN: Yes, but first you'd keep your promise.

THE WITCHES: The promise! The promise!

A WITCH: Return to life!

THE WITCHES: The promise! The promise!

A WITCH: Live! Live!

A DEAD COUSIN: Take this table knife. Bury it in the back of your murderer and Celestino's.

CHORUS OF ELVES: Celestino's! Celestino's!

A COUSIN: Wait, let me sharpen it up a little. (*He sharpens the knife.*) Here you are, nice and sharp. Better yet, bury it in his throat.

THE WITCHES (*enthusiastically, happily, as though, suddenly, they had discovered the saving word*):   His throat! His throat! His throat! (*Their exclamations grow softer and at last fade out. Then the Chorus of Dead Cousins begins.*)

CHORUS OF DEAD COUSINS (*very happily*):   In his throat! In his throat! In his throat! (*Their voices grow softer with each*

Christmas!

— My grandfather

phrase until at the last exclamation they are almost inaudible.)

A WITCH: Now he's alive!

A DEAD COUSIN (*embracing you*):   Be sure to bury it real, real deep. Remember he was the one that killed us all, killed Celestino and killed you and then tried to kill you again.

YOU (*walking on top of the table and clutching the knife in both hands*):   Today we have come back from the mountain very very late. We had so much fun looking for sweetsops and throwing rocks at a lizard that turned a different color every time one hit him. We get home and like always Celestino leaves me at the door. Now my mother will come out and she'll ask me who's killed me.

MOTHER (*stops dancing and runs to the table and hugs you*):   Who has killed you! Who has killed you! (*Rejoins the dance. You throw yourself down on the table.*)

CHORUS OF AUNTS (*never stopping dancing*):   Ay, a husband! Ay, a husband!

YOU (*voice offstage*):   What is this place? This must be where the witches live. You want us to go in? . . . (*Silence.*) Okay, if you don't want to, we won't.

CHORUS OF WITCHES: Come in! Come in!

YOU (*voice offstage*):   Listen to them calling us. We'd better not pay any attention. (*You come closer now, holding the knife, to where your grandfather is dancing.*)

GRANDMOTHER (*to you; still dancing*):   Late coming home again! This time we even ate all the leftovers!

CHORUS OF AUNTS: Spoiled wart! You're too big for us to be always having to scold you!

MOTHER: Ay, this child will be the end of me. I can't take it anymore!

(*You sit down on one of the stools, with the knife hidden behind your back. Now everyone stands motionless, and the only sound heard is the whack whack whack of a hatchet chopping and chopping incessantly.*)

GRANDMOTHER: We're so tired! We better kill him. (*Goes out. The sound of the hatchet continues, then stops.*)

GRANDMOTHER (*entering with the hatchet; to Grandfather*):   Here's the hatchet. Kill him now.

GRANDFATHER: Is it good and sharp?

GRANDMOTHER: Yes.

CHORUS OF AUNTS: Try it first, you don't want to botch it.

GRANDFATHER: Let's try it. Bring me that bird over here to see if I can cut it in half with one whack.

CHORUS OF DEAD COUSINS (*voices offstage*):   Listen, they're right behind us. You better stop that henscratching even if it's just for a second. Let's run!

GRANDMOTHER (*bringing the bird and placing it on the floor*):   Now you'll see whether that hatchet can cut or not.

GRANDFATHER: We'll see—because if it doesn't I'm going to whack you in the head with it.

GRANDMOTHER: Idiot!

(*Grandfather looks furious at Grandmother and tries to hit her with the hatchet, but one of the Aunts steps between them. In the struggle she receives a mortal blow and falls kicking to the floor.*)

GRANDFATHER: Another miserable woman goes to a better life.

THE WITCHES (*coming out of their gloom, grinning sarcastically and shrieking*):   To a better life! To a better life!

CHORUS OF AUNTS: Poor miserable creature, that's how she ends up, like we'll all end up—victims to that beast's hatchet, the beast we have for a father. All our children have already fallen to its blade. We are all damned! And damned to witness this scene without being able to speak a word of protest, or even weep. But now our patience has come to an end. Rather than work like a dog and go on eating messes of corn, I'll go to hell!

THE WITCHES (*reanimated*):   Hell! Hell! Hell!

ONE OF THE AUNTS (*shouting*):   Ay, to be free, even if it's to go to hell!

(*All the Aunts advance with their hands outstretched, palms up.*)

ONE OF THE AUNTS: Look at these hands! Worked to the bones!

TWO AUNTS (*hands extended*):   From breaking rocks my hands are cut to shreds!

ALL THE AUNTS (*hands outstretched farther yet*):   Here are my hands cut to shreds.

AN ELF (*hopping*):   Shreds! Shreds! Shreds!

CHORUS OF AUNTS: Ay!

ELF: Shreds!

CHORUS OF AUNTS: Ay.

ELF: Shreds!

(*The Aunts approach and surround Grandfather and Grandmother. The Dead Aunt stands up and joins the Chorus of Witches.*)

GRANDMOTHER (*frightened; to the circling Aunts*):   What are you going to do to us! What are you going to do to us! Remember, we're your parents!

ONE AUNT (*laughing*):   My parents! (*To the other Aunts.*) Did you hear that! They say they're our parents . . .

CHORUS OF AUNTS (*laughing uproariously. Then they become very serene and begin circling Grandfather and Grandmother*):   Father, Mother—parents—forgive me, but you can hardly expect me to go out to gather dry firewood—I'm having my period.

GRANDFATHER: Nonsense! Nonsense! Don't give me that foolishness! In my time nobody bothered about a little thing like that.

CHORUS OF AUNTS (*as they pin the grandparents against the table*):   The moment has come to pull out their eyes!

GRANDMOTHER: They've all gone crazy! They're drunk!

CHORUS OF AUNTS: The moment has come to pull off their arms!

GRANDMOTHER: Help! Help! They've all gone crazy!

CHORUS OF AUNTS: Look at my hands! Look at my hands! They're cut to shreds! . . .

(*The Aunts seize Grandfather and Grandmother and shake them and bang them against the table. But then Grandfather slips out of their grasp and runs to where the hatchet is lying on the floor. Grandfather begins to slash the hatchet through the air, terrifying the Aunts and laughing loudly.)*

GRANDFATHER: You think it's so easy to pull out my eyes and kill me, huh! Well think again—I'm too old an old prick to be taken by surprise. I plan to live a hundred years! Maybe more! . . . No one in this house will escape me! I'm in charge! *I'm* holding the hatchet again! I could split all your skulls like green calabashes. But I won't—you'll have to serve me, and obey me, and die when I say so. *(To Grandmother, also trembling over with the Aunts.)* Bring me that bird over here so I can try out this hatchet.

(Grandmother picks up the bird. From very far away seems to come the murmur of an unending clamor, with boys' laughter, voices, singing—the great noise of many children playing in the country. You advance with the knife held high, and one of the Elves steps in ahead of you to shield you—that way you are hidden from the living.)

GRANDFATHER *(to Grandmother)*: Put it there on the floor!

(One of the Witches takes the bird away from Grandmother and places it on the floor.)

CHORUS OF DEAD COUSINS *(voices offstage, singing)*:

> Sally, Sally Wallflower, come sprinkle your plants,
> For down in the meadow there lies a young man.
> Rise, Sally, rise, and don't you look sad,
> For you shall have a husband, good or bad.
> Choose you one, choose you two,
> Choose the nicest you can see!

(Grandfather raises the hatchet.)

CHORUS OF WITCHES: The moment has come! At last Celestino will be rescued and return to us!

I AM MY FATE.

LET ME WEEP!

— Songs of the Caravan

I come to speak

YOUR NAME

so I may begin
this dream again.

— Garden of Caresses

A WITCH: To us!
CHORUS OF DEAD COUSINS: Celestino! Celestino!

(*All the Elves run around and around and back and forth in the dining room. They climb up on the table. They hop about. They stand on the stools. They dance with each other. They are not still for even an instant. Grandfather raises the hatchet higher and gets ready to cut off the dead bird's head. The Elf protecting you from the living people's sight stands aside and leaves your front exposed. You raise the knife to the height of Grandfather's back.*)

GRANDMOTHER: The knife!

(*Grandfather quickly turns. He looks at you. You are still holding the knife high over your head. You are about to stab him in the face. Grandfather smiles at you. The knife falls to the floor. The Chorus of Dead Cousins shouts and screams. Grandfather turns his back to you and chops off the head of the dead bird. The dining room door opens and Celestino comes in. He is invisible. You walk over to him, put your arm around his shoulders, and say:*)

YOU (*with one arm in the air*):   Forgive me for not being able to save you. Forgive me, but when I was going to stab him in the face, he looked at me and smiled . . .
CHORUS OF DEAD COUSINS: He looked at me and smiled. At *me*. Nobody ever smiled at me before.
YOU (*arm still hanging in mid-air*):   He looked at me and he smiled at me. And I just couldn't do it anymore.
CHORUS OF DEAD COUSINS: He looked at me and he smiled at me—at *me*. I'm used to them not doing anything but kicking me in the behind and chopping at my back with the hatchet.

(*You become more and more a part of the group of Dead Cousins. Arm always raised, embracing Celestino.*)

THE WITCHES: Now the only thing we can do is go away with the dead cousins. Now there is nothing left to look for or try to achieve. Grandfather just cut down the last tree. Now, where will we be able to write that unending poem, which has not even begun to be written? We are exposed to the sun, and it is even possible that for a long long time night will not even fall. (*They mix with the Chorus of Dead Cousins.*)

GRANDMOTHER (*stops dancing; to Mother, who stands motionless, looking out the window towards the pasture*): Don't be such a goose, woman! Don't you see he's better off this way.

(*Mother is still in a daze. She doesn't seem to have heard a thing.*)

CHORUS OF AUNTS: It's better this way. And especially when you consider what a poet for a son would have gotten you . . .

GRANDFATHER: And a half-wit! Because he was a half-wit. Every time you sent him to bring the calves in he always left one or two of them out there lost somewhere. And he never did things the way they ought to have been done. If you told him, "Go out and pick up some kindling," as likely as not he'd pull up a whole shower-of-gold tree and drag it in . . .

AN AUNT: If you sent him for water, he spilled it all by the time he'd stumbled halfway back.

GRANDMOTHER: When you sent him to move the cows, he'd set them to grazing on the spurge and crown of thorns . . .

CHORUS OF AUNTS: He was useless! He was useless! He spent his whole life scribbling on the tree trunks and putting dirty words and filth all over them.

MOTHER: What a disgrace! My God, what a disgrace!

GRANDMOTHER: It was all your fault for spoiling him! Instead of a man what you got was . . . trash!

CHORUS OF AUNTS: Trash! Trash! Trash!

GRANDFATHER: He was useless. He didn't earn enough to pay for his own breakfast.

CHORUS OF AUNTS: Useless! He was useless trash!

GRANDMOTHER: And how embarrassing—everybody knew he was a poet . . .

CHORUS OF AUNTS: How embarrassing! How embarrassing! I'd like to crawl in a hole from the embarrassment.

AN ELF (*doing tumbling tricks across the table on one leg*): "My name is Noboddy, and my mother, my father and all my friends all call me Noboddy . . ."

ANOTHER ELF (*hopping up and down and doing acrobatics on the table, on one leg; comes over to first elf and slaps him*): Homer, ninth book of the *Odyssey*.

AN AUNT: How peaceful this house is now, after we torched that wasp-nest!

MOTHER: Now I'll have to carry water to water the plants with all by myself . . .

CHORUS OF DEAD COUSINS: January has reappeared to me. Or maybe it's just my imagination . . . I can't tell the difference anymore between what I see and what I imagine I see. But I'm almost sure he appeared again. He came all the way to where Celestino and I were lying on the grass and eating earthworms, and he said to us, "You'll get your memory back soon," then he didn't say anything for a minute, and then he spoke to us again. "As soon as you remember the word you forgot, you'll have nice, sound, peaceful sleep again." That's what he told us, and I saw him rise up into the clouds and disappear off behind those mountains. And from way, way off there I heard him say, "You'll remember the word soon." "You'll remember the word soon."

A VOICE (*offstage*): Did you hear what January told us?

ANOTHER VOICE (*offstage*): What did you say?

A VOICE: Oh, you're still asleep . . .

CHORUS OF DEAD COUSINS (*imitating the first voice*): I'm sure I heard someone talking. It can't all be imagined. At least I'm sure Celestino is asleep close by and that he has a little fever. It's very bad to have a fever when you live like we live—here in the middle of the plains with the rain falling right down on top of us. I go to the pasture and without coming too close to the house I cut some mint and wormseed leaves to make him some tea. But then I realize I don't have any matches to start a fire with. If I could only go up to the house and steal some matches from Grandma. But I'll never set foot in that house again, because I know they're all up there waiting for me, to jump on me with both feet. I'll give him the leaves without cooking them.

GRANDMOTHER (*looking out the window*): The boys certainly take their own sweet time coming back from the river! . . .

MOTHER (*impatient*): Why do you say that! It's still early . . .

CHORUS OF AUNTS: Tell me what time it is! Tell me what time it is!

AN ELF (*doing tumbling tricks across the table and breaking plates*): "Arrived from other places you will go everywhere."

SECOND ELF (*with a plate on his head*): Arthur Rimbaud, *Une Saison en Enfer.*

(*Great noise of hatchets like a hard rain falling among the trees. There are moments when the sound grows intolerable. Then it moves off, until it completely fades away.*)

CHORUS OF DEAD COUSINS: I've asked Celestino why he'd never just exploded, and rebelled against his family. I told him if he wanted me to, I'd help him. I've told him if he wants me to I can pull out the stake that Grandpa drove through his heart. I've offered to take the stake and go up to the house and drive it through the old man's heart while he was sleeping. But he's always said it doesn't hurt him the least little bit, and that he's not going to rebel.

A VOICE (*offstage, heard through the noise of distant hatchets*): But if you're in the right, why not rebel?

ANOTHER VOICE: Because I'm not that sure that I'm right.

FIRST VOICE: But you're innocent . . .

SECOND VOICE: I don't know about that . . .

FIRST VOICE: Well, then, are they the ones that aren't crazy?

SECOND VOICE: That's possible.

FIRST VOICE: So if they're the ones that are right, why don't you say "I'm sorry" and get on their side?

SECOND VOICE: Because I can't do that.

CHORUS OF WITCHES (*shouting*): I can't do that!

AN ELF (*breaking almost all the plates*): "I can't do that!"

CHORUS OF ELVES (*unsure of themselves; circumspect*): Anonymous . . . Untitled . . . ?

THE KINDNESS
OF SILENCE!

— The Magic Mirror

(Boy's weeping offstage. Then someone calls to the cows in the pasture.)

CHORUS OF WITCHES (*reciting in chorus*):   "I will see you again in a few days. It is impossible for me to believe that the dawn is so near. Within a few days I will listen to your voice and drink from your mouth that water that makes me forget my insatiable thirst.

"I was like the calf which has lost its mother.

"I was like the butterfly which can no longer find the only flower whose nectar nourishes.

"Incessantly I pronounce your name and that of the son you have given me. How can the heart of a man contain a love such as this!

"Think of the millions of years that have been necessary for the rain, the wind, the rivers, and the sea to make of a rock that handful of sand you are playing with.

"Think of the thousands of beings that have been necessary for your lips to be warm under my kisses.

"As the pilgrim makes ablutions with the sand, I raise in my hands two handfuls of this golden dust you play with, and shower it over my back.

"I will see you again in a few days."

CHORUS OF DEAD COUSINS: Celestino is dead inside the cage. Even if I can't see him, I know that he's dead. The witch has been doing somersaults in the air, and she told me, "He's dead." But I didn't pay any attention, I just kept on picking cactus flowers and grape ivy shoots to make him tea and bring down his fever. "He's dead," one of the ivy shoots told me when I reached to break it off. But I didn't pay any attention, I just broke it off . . . I come to the house with my hands full of ivy vines and leaves and flowers from all the plants I've come across. My mother comes running out to meet me and she says, "He's dead." "He's dead."

CHORUS OF WITCHES: "Free me, O powerful prudence, free me from loving without hope, for that is madness."

CHORUS OF COUSINS: I will never go back home anymore, where my mother always waits for me, crying under the Indian laurel tree. And I will never peep down into the well again, because I'm afraid of seeing myself—like that other time—down there in the bottom. I will never go to the house anymore. I'll never go get another bucket of water. And I'll never pay any mind to Grandpa again when he tells me to stand in front of the calves or fillies and hold them still . . . I'm just going to lie down here in the grass with all the chiggers in it and wait for the rains to come and float me away on a boiling stream to where they say he lay down to drown . . .

CHORUS OF AUNTS: Ay, ay, the last time they ever saw him they say he was running around naked.

GRANDFATHER: Ay, ay, and with his feet raw and blistered.

MOTHER: Ay, ay, and writing and writing and never stopping . . .

CHORUS OF WITCHES: "I cannot go to sleep before the dawn.
"This morning the thought of it brings me joy.
"My solitude is peopled with a thousand presences . . ."

CHORUS OF AUNTS (*leaving in a group, followed by Grandfather, Grandmother, and Mother*): It looks like the boys are finally coming back from the river. Let's go out and meet them and give them each four whacks on their backsides. We'll teach them—they can't leave the house without our permission.

(*Grandfather bawls like a calf as he walks towards the door. Mother stands stock-still in the middle of the dining room. Grandmother tries to drag her with her, but she can't so she finally gives up and goes out hopping on just one leg.*)

YOU (*among the Chorus of Dead Cousins*): I went to the well, and when I peeked into the bottom I saw my mother smiling all cheerful at me from the water.

CHORUS OF WITCHES: Smiling all cheerful at me from the water.

YOUR VOICE (*from the bottom of the well*): Everything is so calm and peaceful here. If you only knew how very very calm and peaceful. Celestino is here with me, too. Celestino, my mother, and me here in this watery bottom, where nobody dares peek for fear of seeing us. And people that pass by say, "That well is haunted. I've heard voices down at the bottom of it." And I hear them run off and I feel so happy, and little by little, hugging my mother and Celestino, I fall asleep.

Asleep, and always floating on this water that looks to me like it's turning smelly green.

(Mother brings her hands to her face. She disappears from the dining room. Immediately she enters again, emitting loud laughter that sounds as though it were coming from the bottom of a well. She goes to the table and gobbles down a large hunk of plantain in one mouthful. Then she begins to walk on all fours. She exits the dining room in that position. Grandmother follows her movements as though she were completely unreal. Grandmother will walk with military strides, one hand at her throat and the other stretched in front of her, as though rehearsing some exotic ritual dance.)

YOU *(advancing imaginarily towards Celestino)*: Come on, let's play hopscotch. Don't you like to play hopscotch?

(All the Cousins start playing hopscotch. They hop, turn around, bump into one another. For a second we have an unreal vision. Mother crosses the dining room, raising and lowering her skirt, disappearing off the other side.)

CHORUS OF WITCHES: "Do not wake me if I am fortunate enough to sleep at the hour the birds begin to coo.
"For me all dawns are pale under my cover of green silk."
ALL THE ELVES *(gathered at one corner of the dining room)*: Pale! Pale! Pale!
CHORUS OF WITCHES: "Far-off sounds scrape painfully across the silence.
"I do not even feel curious to know how many buds have opened on the plum tree.
"But nonetheless, it is meet to get up . . ."
ALL THE ELVES: Get up! Get up!

(Grandfather crosses the room with the hatchet on his shoulder, wiping the sweat off his face. Behind him, Grandmother conversing with Death and carrying an empty cage. All the Cousins jump and hop about, as they play hopscotch. Their noise and laughter also comes in from outside . . .)

CHORUS OF WITCHES: "In the Palace of Crystal, chrysan-
themums flower for the fairies and elves and the poet
clearly perceives those flowers, which have the appearance
of chalices hewn from agate."

ALL THE ELVES (*as they disappear off all sides of the dining
room*): Agate! Agate!

(*The Aunts cross the room, hands in the air, stepping to the
beat of an unheard military march. They march with firm
but surreal steps.*)

CHORUS OF DEAD COUSINS (*voices offstage*): There comes Celestino carrying a dead grass snake.

CHORUS OF AUNTS (*voices offstage*): That snake is swallowing
Celestino up like he was a frog.

(*Distant laughter and singing are heard.*)

MOTHER (*voice offstage*): Goddamned child! You've fallen down
another time, have you, on the way back—so you come home
with the buckets empty! You deserve a whipping! . . .

GRANDFATHER (*voice offstage*): He's a half-wit! He's a half-wit!
And the only thing he knows how to do is spend the livelong
day scribbling and carving on the trees and writing filth.

(*Laughter and singing again.*)

GRANDMOTHER (*voice shrieking offstage*): Run! Run! She's
jumped in the well!

(*Complete silence. Then a great shouting and screaming of
children and a hubbub of unintelligible jabbering. The
Cousins from the dining room, playing hopscotch, continue.
You will become more and more a part of their group, as
though one more member of the Chorus of the Dead.*)

CHORUS OF WITCHES (*moving towards the window. As the Chorus of Witches speaks, Grandmother's shouts of "She's
jumped in the well!" will be heard, but very distantly,*

almost inaudible): "Do not wake me if I am fortunate enough to sleep at the hour the birds begin their cooing. For me all dawns are pale under my coverlet of green silk. Their murmurs scratch painfully across the silence. So much the worse for the early-morning visitor who awaits me in the hall. I do not even feel curious to know how many buds have opened on the plum tree. Nonetheless, it is meet for me to arise . . . The smoke from chimneys draws arabesques above the roofs.

"I try to decipher in the streaked firmament a message of love.

"Very soon those drawings will disperse.

"And now the sky is implacably naked.

"Somber before the window I contemplate the garden where the wind flutters the leaves.

"Spring is late, but the grass of sorrow grows green in all seasons."

(*The shouts of Grandmother end. The Chorus of Aunts stands unmoving at the window, looking out enchanted into the yard. Silence. And then suddenly the calm is broken by a great shout of boys, heard playing, singing, asking each other riddles, running all about. We are in the country and the boys are having fun playing. At intervals the muffled sound of a hatchet is heard, and then the echoing fall of a tree that crashes, shakes the whole mountain, and sets in motion long waves of echoes. Then the voices, the hullabaloo continue.*)

I've run out here to the stand of wild pineapples with a bottle of wine to hide in those prickly leaves, so I can get drunk in peace later, with nobody to bother me. It feels so wonderful to get drunk and lie on your back on the ground! You don't even feel the fire ants biting you . . . I really like to get drunk—so I'm going to try to hide all the bottles I can. I'll go back to the house and bring some more wine to hide in the hollows of the wild pineapple plants.

I've already made more than twenty trips back and forth and

every time I've brought all sorts of wine, and even a bottle of crème de menthe that Grandma had hidden for herself. When she finds out she'll scream bloody murder. But to hell with her— if I didn't steal it, one of my aunts would, because they're the kind that always say, "Oh, look what I found!" and steal everything they lay eyes on, and some things they don't even lay eyes on, just *hands*, in the dark. At my mother's wedding, since she's such a goose and lets everybody and his uncle take advantage of her, they practically had her in her birthday suit—they stole all her clothes, which weren't all that much to begin with, and now my mother has to wear burlap or floursack skirts and cover herself with whatever she can make shift out of. Goddamned miserable aunts!

And as though that weren't enough, all they do is pick on me and make fun of me and call me names. I'm tired of it—one of these days I'm going to take me a little poison and put it in their food, so even the cat will get his. Uh-huh, that's what I'm going to do one day, but first I'll have to warn my mother and decide on the day, so she won't go and taste the food. And they'll see—there won't even be a cat left in the house! . . . It looks like my aunts have discovered that the twenty bottles of wine are missing, since I can hear a racket in the house to set your hair on end. It sounds like they're blaming poor Celestino, since they're giving him a hiding that sounds like they're murdering him. You can hear him yelling from here. Yelling and yelling.

"Stop hitting Celestino! It was me! I'm the one that stole the wine!"

Now a whole swarm of people is after me—all my aunts, with sticks and stones, and my goddamned old grandma, who other times just complains but doesn't do a thing but this time is chasing me like she was a fifteen-year-old girl instead of a rickety old woman. Old biddy! Even if you poison my mother, I guarantee I'll poison *you!* Here comes Grandpa too, swinging the hatchet around above his head and cursing a blue streak. I've got to figure out a way to escape from these damned people, because if they catch me, as drunk as they all are, they'll chop me up into toothpicks and sausage stuffing.

·   ·   ·

As far as

I'm concerned,

there's nothing like

MEATBALLS!

— One of my aunts

Here comes a candle to light
you to bed. And here comes
a hatchet to chop off your head.

— Children's rhyme

Grandpa's hatchet whizzed by my head and it practically struck sparks. They've almost got me hemmed in now. I wish I could fly! But wouldn't you know it, no matter how much I need to, I just can't, and I don't see a witch anywhere around now. I'll have to manage the best I can by myself.

Now they grab me by the arms and try to pull me apart, like quartering a chicken. One of my aunts gives me a whack on the head that sounds like somebody thumped a watermelon. And Grandma, the goddamned old biddy, is beating me with a piece of fence paling.

"I'll never tell where the bottles are stashed! I'm not going to say a word, so you may as well get it over with and kill me!"

"Ungrateful child!"

"How is it possible that not even on a holy day like today is there a moment's peace in this house? Somebody ought to pull the little brat's head off!"

"I'll kill him!"

"Where did you hide those bottles?"

"I'll never tell!"

Grandpa shakes me till my eyes rattle and then starts in kicking me. But I'm as stubborn as a fence post, so even if he kills me I won't tell. Grandpa gets tired of shaking me, so he picks up the hatchet and holds it and says to me—

"Now you're going to tell me where you hid those bottles, because if you don't I'm going to split your head like a gourd."

"Take the hatchet away from the man, he's drunk!"

"He's gone crazy!"

"The hatchet!"

Grandpa swipes at me with the hatchet, but it just grazes my ear and keeps going. It takes off his big toe, though. Grandpa lets out a whinny like a horse when they cut off his oysters and I grab my chance and take off running while Grandma makes the sign of the cross about ten times in the air and two witches lift me up into the air and carry me off and hide me as far away in the old pineapple stand as we can get . . . The crowd of lizards sunning on top of the pile of bottles run off when they see me coming with the witches. Now it's time for *our* party. One of the witches opens the first bottle and tilts it up. Not one to be left behind, I open the second bottle. And the third. And the fourth.

And the fifth . . . Four lizards dressed all in white went off to the other side of the river and set themselves on fire, so they say.

> Rockaby baby in the treetop,
> When the wind blows the cradle will rock.
> When the bough breaks the cradle will fall,
> And down will come baby, cradle and all.

Some lizards go past, shooting off sparks and singing in chorus. Then they take off flying and perch up on the Indian laurel tree where one night Grandma when she was going out to the outhouse found Grandpa, stiff as a board, swinging on the end of a rope that had him by the neck. "What a sad way to go," Grandma said that night as she went into the privy, all wrapped up in a sheet. "My father hanged himself from that Indian laurel tree too," she said, "and my father-in-law and my grandfather, and me, and now the old man. What a sad way to go! I'm going to cut that tree down first thing tomorrow."

But she never did.

Mama's found my hiding place and comes up to me with her eyes full of tears.

"Son," she says, "give me those bottles of wine to take back to the house. Stop pestering, now. Don't try me anymore. I'm so, so miserable, now . . ."

That was the way my mother talked to me, and when she said the word *miserable* her voice got more choked up than usual, and I actually thought she was going to go dumb.

Mama is an old woman now. An old woman who's never been able to face the fact that she's an old woman, because there are people older than she is at home.

My mother always takes a backseat in everything, the one that waits till everybody else eats to eat herself. The one that sleeps in the backmost bedroom, next to the corn press full of rats. Since she doesn't have her own house or husband, my mother has had to bring up all my cousins and midwife at all my aunts' lying-ins. But my aunts treat her like dirt and say she's a fool. My cousins kick dirt in her face too and call her dotty and senile and things, and sometimes I say the same things to her. Poor Mama! The man that left her should've died before he did it.

I've given all the bottles to my mother. I'll have to wait till next year to go on my binge . . . I've given all the bottles to my mother, and all of a sudden I start feeling happy. I watch her go off and I say to myself, I certainly hope I haven't made another mistake! I hope this woman is really my mother. I hope I'm not making all this up, and my real mother's not waiting for me up at the house with a piece of kindling. But no—I've never invented a person that could say *miserable* the way my mother just said it. Yes, I shouldn't have any doubt—even if it was for just a few seconds, I've just seen my mother for the first time. Now I don't care if the other one takes a kindling stick to my head.

My mother is the youngest woman there is.
My mother is so young that I can carry her with me anywhere at all.
My mother is smart.
My mother tells me a different story every single night.
My mother sings like nobody ever sang before.
My mother is my mother.
My mother knows how to shinny up palm trees.
My mother can swim on top of the water.
My mother took me to see the sun last night.
My mother is cleaning house.
My mother is dancing on the roof.
My mother is singing in the bottom of the well.
My mother is meowing in the parlor.
My mother is raffling off a dress.
My mother is begging for pennies with a cup.
My mother is knocking at the door.

My mother is closing my eyes.
Listen to my mother cleaning house.
Listen to my mother dancing on the roof.
Listen to my mother meowing in the parlor.
Listen to my mother raffling off a dress.
Listen to my mother begging for pennies with a cup.
Listen to my mother knocking at the door.
Listen to my mother singing in the bottom of the well.
Singing in the bottom of the well.
Singing in the bottom of the well.
Singing in the bottom of the well.
Listen to my mother singing in the bottom of the well.
Listen to my mother closing my eyes.
Closing my eyes.
Closing my eyes.
Closing my eyes.

It's been such a pretty day today. Early in the morning the cockroaches peeped into my castle and said, "Hail." I ran out the big door, my eyes full of tears, and I started singing. The cockroaches bowed, all so respectfully, and then I broke out laughing . . . They've taken my arm and we're walking through the pasture. What sun! What tremendous glare! Without noticing, we've almost melted. But still, how cool! It feels like we were in one of those early December or January mornings—what nice months! But they're so short! We've walked right through the big mudholes there are on the other side of the river. But we've hardly gotten muddy at all. The cockroaches pick me up and carry me by my hands and feet and I say, "How polite!" "How polite!" But the strangest thing is that they haven't gotten dirty either—their shells shine in the sunshine like custard apple skins and sometimes they get so pretty, with all their legs in the air, that I hug them and say, "Don't leave me!" "Don't leave me!" . . . But they've never even thought for a second about leaving me—"We'll follow you anywhere," they've said, and I get such a chill that I feel my stomach start knotting up and the chill run up and down me like it'll never stop. We jump across the river in one hop and lie down to rest on a great big elephant-ear leaf. But then we walk some more, because it'll be night pretty soon and then what's to keep them from stomping our guts out? . . .

The cockroaches have gone off and left me all alone. Right in the middle of our walk they turn my arm loose and say, "You tricked us. You said you were one of us, but we just found out you're eternal." Eternal?, I ask, but they'd already disappeared. "Eternal"—some shiny green-and-purple blackbirds flying way way up high said that. I took off flying after them, to try to catch up to them. But they disappeared right before my eyes. So I came back down to earth.

For the first time I felt lonesomer than I'd ever felt before.

If you didn't exist, I'd have to invent you. So I invent you. And instantly that makes me not feel so lonesome. But all of a sudden the elephants and fish come up. And they grab me by the neck and pull out my tongue. And they wind up convincing me to make myself eternal.

So, I have to try to invent something again. Until finally there's not a tree left standing. Now I can sleep easy, with my big hatchet tucked under my arm.

I've come back to the yard again. Chased by thousands of different-sized lizards and some of them with lots of heads that butt me and bite me. What could I do but come back to the yard. But would you look at this—the lizards come right up to the well and jump over it with one hop and keep on coming till they almost catch up with me.

And then they do catch me. And knock me over. And little by little tear me to pieces.
Celestino!
Celestino!
Celestino!

"Wake up, you all, Celestino has died."

. . .

I picked him up and carried him to the graveyard. But my cousins didn't want me to bury him next to where they were. So I had to eat him so the buzzards wouldn't. That's why they're so mean and mad now and fly way way up there in the clouds, to get a good start and dive straight down at me and peck Celestino out of my stomach. But they're not going to be able to manage that—I'm too close to the door. I drag myself just a little bit farther and make it to the house.

"Madre mía! Open the door—there's a flock of buzzards right behind me! Open up! Open up!"

My mother has opened the door for me but she's standing there so I can't get in.

"Let me in!"

"No, you can't yet."

"If I don't get in the buzzards and lizards are going to eat me up."

"You know very well it's not on your account the buzzards are flying up there so high, and it's not you the lizards want to eat—you are eternal."

"No!"

"I'm telling you, and I'm your mother, and I know because I'm eternal too. Both of us have to suffer that fate—it's the most terrible fate there is."

My mother has slammed the door in my face and has gone into the parlor sobbing. Grandpa is asleep with the hatchet under him, and Grandma is making all sorts of faces in the air, but she doesn't so much as dare peep out through the cracks in the wall . . . They say at night I still go outside and walk to the well and stand there real still, looking into the bottom, and that one time my mother grabbed me, just as I climbed up on the wellhead palings made out of naked-boy tree saplings . . .

I come to the Indian laurel tree—the only one still standing—and bump into the elf.

"I've finally seen what you want," I say to him, "but now there's nothing I can do to give you the ring."

"It doesn't matter. I don't need it anymore anyway."

"Why not?"

The rain
in the night
does truly
sing.

— Eliseo Diego

"Somebody you know stole it from you and gave it to me before you knew you had it. That's why I've gone on asking you for it—I've come to you just so I could do you some good. So you would think about things and realize what you don't see but that sees you. Things you don't even suspect or sense but that rule you. And bewilder you. But you've been pigheaded—so now you're condemned to eternity. All I can do now is wish you patience—more patience than I, who am also one of the eternal ones, have ever had or ever will have."

"But why didn't you tell me you were out to help me?"

"You never paid any mind to me, and every time I got close to you, you tried to imagine you were dreaming. It was so incredible to you that somebody could just for no reason try to give you a helping hand! Is it that you don't trust anything you can't put your hands on?—and your hands, I'll tell you, are a lot less real than any of my legends. But it's too late now—here are the leaves. If you want me to, I'll show you the ring. Here—it's just like any other ring. Except this one was yours and now you'll never be able to get it back again."

The elf was slowly disappearing above the highest branches of the Indian laurel tree. For a few seconds the ring glittered among the leaves, and I wished I knew whether I'd ever be able to come across it again.

"Since we're eternal," I said to the elf, "tell me your name—that way I'll know what to call you someday, in a thousand years or so, or a thousand centuries or so, wherever and whenever we meet again."

"My name is Celestino," he said.

And he suddenly vanished above the highest bud on the tree.

Seven times already I've knocked on the door. I've come back naked this time, and I must be old—maybe horrible. My mother has come to open the door, with Grandpa and Grandma right behind.

"What is it?" my mother asks.

"I want to stay with you tonight," I say. "It's raining outside and by the way it looks there's a fistful of lightning claps ready to throw themselves right on my head."

"You can't tonight, no," my mother said, and I saw the tears trying to come out of her eyes.

Grandma and Grandpa smiled quickly and then their faces went back to usual.

"When can I?"

"Tomorrow! Come tomorrow!"—and I could hear how her throat was tightening up on her. "Come tomorrow!" my mother said again as Grandpa broke the hatchet in half and Grandma looked up towards the roof—trying to find a crack to escape out of. "Tomorrow!" she said again, and finally she turned into a giant owl moth from down by the river. One of those that just come out when it's rained a lot and keeps on raining.

There was an Indian laurel tree outside. Two or three crickets going whirrr whirrr whirrr. A chorus of witches having a conversation up on the roof of the house. And me. I lay down on my back on the squishy-wet ground and very happily started counting, by twos, the different clouds that floated past underneath my eyes and that once in a while made me a real complicated signal.

Then I thought that the faster I went to sleep the sooner the next day would come. And I fell right asleep. And I slept.

And I slept.

And they say I sleepwalked to the well and climbed up on top of the wellhead. And that I stood there waiting like the other time for my mother to grab me just as I was about to teeter over and fall into the hole.

But going by what they just now told me, that night my mother didn't get there in time. But I've got my own opinion— I'm pretty sure she got there too soon.

THE LAST END